GOOD MEN AND GRACE

A Novel

Alita Maria Ngo
with
Robert J. Irish

*To Estrellita,
my best friend!
God bless you in
His love with endless
graces.
Love,
Alita*

Published by
Full Quiver Publishing
Pakenham ON Canada

This book is a work of fiction.
Characters and incidents are products of the
author's imagination.

Good Men and Grace
Copyright 2022 Alita Ngo

Published by
Full Quiver Publishing
PO Box 244
Pakenham, Ontario K0A 2X0
www.fullquiverpublishing.com

ISBN Number: 978-1-987970-33-3
Printed and bound in the USA
Cover design: James Hrkach
Cover photo copyright:
235573635 © Outdoorsman | Dreamstime.com

NATIONAL LIBRARY OF CANADA
CATALOGUING IN PUBLICATION

Published by FQ Publishing
A Division of Innate Productions

For Mamita

Dedicated to Jim
without whom this story
never would have found its voice

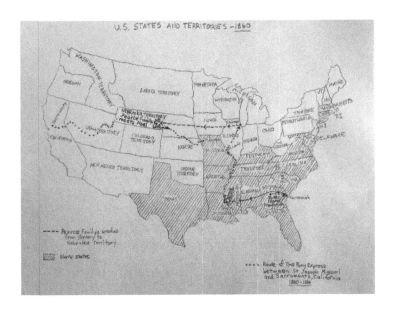

U.S. STATES AND TERRITORIES - 1860

- - - Pearce Family's exodus from Slavery to Nebraska Territory

▨ Slave states

···· Route of The Pony Express between St. Joseph, Missouri and Sacramento, California 1860-1861

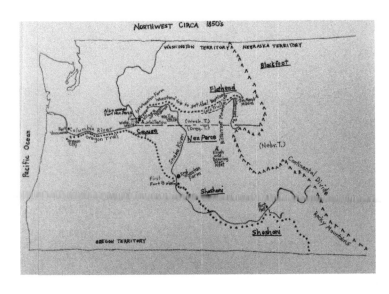

NORTHWEST CIRCA 1850's

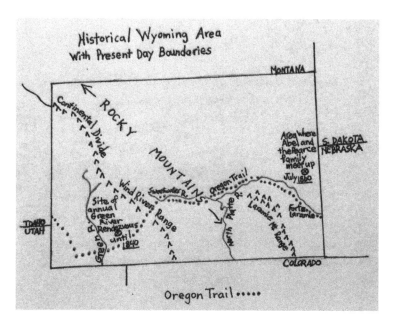

Historical Wyoming Area
With Present Day Boundaries

MONTANA

ROCKY

Continental Divide

MOUNTAINS

Area where
Abel and
the Pearce
family
meet up
⊗
July 1850

S. DAKOTA
NEBRASKA

Sweetwater R.

Oregon Trail!

Wind River Range

Site of
annual
Green
River
Rendezvous
until
1840

North Platte R.

Fort Laramie

Laramie Mt. Range

IDAHO
UTAH

Green

COLORADO

Oregon Trail •••••

Day unto day takes up the story and night unto night makes known the message.
Psalm 19: 2

In the tender compassion of our God
the dawn from on high shall break upon us,
to shine on those who dwell in darkness
and the shadow of death,
and to guide our feet into the way of peace.
Luke 1: 78-79

CHAPTER ONE

Nineteen-year-old Abel Wheaton was one of 186 riders of the Pony Express mail service. Secured across the seat of his saddle was the mochila, or mail pouch, collected three days earlier by another rider in St. Joseph, Missouri; it had been passed on to several other riders and delivered about an hour ago to the Pony Express station in Fort Laramie. On this early July morning of 1860, Abel galloped toward his final destination, another station about 125 miles west on the High Plains desert of the future state of Wyoming.

Dressed in brown buckskin pants and shirt, cowboy boots, and a slouch hat, he was protected from the wind and sun about as well as he could be; and, lashed with buckskin ties behind his saddle, he carried an Indian-made wool poncho to wear in the event of summer rains.

The stations had been laid out roughly ten miles apart, so Abel was only about two miles from the first of the stations on his route when he caught the fast movement of a band of Cheyenne Indians out of the corner of his eye. Looking to his right, he immediately decided the fast-approaching Indians did not have friendship and fellowship in mind. Pony Express riders were equipped only with a handgun–usually, a Colt six-shooter revolver to save weight–allowing the horses to run faster

1

and farther. That weapon would not be much of a defense against marauding Indians. Just their number alone would overwhelm a single rider even if he were more heavily armed. Instead, the rider had to rely on the speed of his mount and his ability to outwit them.

Now facing such a situation, Abel fired three shots at the Indians to delay their charge momentarily; as he sped on, he lashed his horse across the neck and rump with the reins. The horse had plainly sensed the danger, and adrenaline spurred him a bit faster. Fortunately, the Indians, in their rush down the hillside, evidently had misjudged the angle of interception, so when they reached the bottom of the hill, they were a full fifty yards behind Abel and his horse. Still, Abel's salvation lay at the first Pony Express station west of Fort Laramie, but it was well over a mile away. The Indian ponies, of course, were much fresher than his horse, but the Pintos were smaller and not as fast, so Abel hoped to outrace them.

He was in the horse race of his life, however, and losing it was not a practical option. He hunkered down in the saddle to evade any arrows sent his way and urged his mount forward. The Indians regained speed on the flat ground along the trail and perceptively crept up to Abel and his horse. Several of them, with their horses at a gallop, fired arrows at Abel, but all fell short or wide of their mark. Even for Indians well experienced in archery, shooting from a galloping horse was an "iffy proposition" at best but did have the adverse

2

effect for the Indians of pressing Abel not to loiter!

At last, the station came in sight. The station master and several visiting ranchers must have heard the shrill yelling of the Indians and were firing their rifles as soon as they were in view on the trail. Before they were in range of the rifle fire, however, the Indians obviously decided the better part of valor was to abandon the chase, so they veered off into the hills to the north and disappeared. The Indians' whoops were replaced by the shouts of the station master and the ranchers, who chose not to leave the safety of the station to chase after the Indians. Even though they were well-armed with rifles, they were outnumbered about five to one.

Undeterred, Abel immediately transferred the mail pouch to a fresh, saddled horse from the station corral, sprang to his mount, and was off at a gallop again. The remaining trip was uneventful unless Abel counted the lightning and driving rainstorm that threatened to incinerate or drown him and his horse near the sixth station. Or the drunk station master at the eighth station, who had forgotten to saddle a fresh horse, so Abel lost ten minutes doing that himself.

That night, having completed his section of the run on the 1900-mile route from western Missouri to Sacramento, California, Abel rested at the tenth station, reflecting on his life so far: his joint Anglo and Indian birthright derived from his father, Elijah, and his mother, Dancing

Star; and their deaths and his orphan status since then, unbroken, except for a time, by the care and love of his Nez Perce grandfather. Thoughts of his parents and past events were coming more often in recent weeks to disturb Abel, not only when he stopped to rest but even as he rode hard and fast across the dusty Wyoming terrain.

He thought he finally had learned to be comfortable with himself after a childhood and youth of sometimes brutal threats from those who busied themselves with branding the outside of a person rather than taking account of what was inside. He was not completely at home in either the Indian camps or in the towns of the settlers, for many in each place derided this "half-breed" as an inferior—and that was not to change in his lifetime.

Abel was ready for his few, well-earned, and welcome leave days that would begin the next day. His mood brightened at the thought of being rejoined with Artemis, the gray-dappled-white Appaloosa horse given to him by his grandfather, Laughing Thunder, a Nez Perce leader. Artemis was Abel's most prized possession, and he always looked forward to riding her again when he returned to Fort Laramie, his home since the beginning of May that year.

When a replacement rider had been called for on the stretch he now rode, Abel was in the right place at the right time, switching promptly to his present run. Before that, he rode the trail's 130-mile route further west through the Sierra

Nevada into Sacramento. Abel had initially been constrained, out of the company's necessity, to relocate to Carson City, Nevada, and to travel that more challenging part of the trail when he was first employed as a Pony Express rider over three months before. His present route suited Abel better all around, leading him from and back to the headquarters, where he felt more at home than anywhere else in the past three years.

CHAPTER TWO

Sunlight came to the first full day of Abel's eagerly anticipated vacation. About a day's slow-paced ride north of Fort Laramie, he watched the dawn spread its palette of pinks and blues above the horizon to the east as the sun rose over the High Plains desert. He had camped by a creek at the foot of a low hill on the plains the night before. Dressed in deerskin pants, jacket, and a woolen shirt, he was mounted upon Artemis and had his six-gun in his holster and a rifle in a scabbard attached to his saddle.

Abel gazed into the soft rose glow crowning the distant peaks. At five feet, eight inches tall, he possessed the slender build and light weight necessary to be hired by the Pony Express; what he lacked in bulk and stature, he made up for in the hearty strength and endurance that came to him naturally from his prior occupations of farming, hunting, and ranching. With features that belied his mixed heritage— the attractive high cheekbones of his mother, the narrower Celtic nose of his father, and a light olive complexion deepened by the sun's tanning—Abel was considered a handsome young man. His light-brown eyes and the manner that morning of his long, drifting, dark, hair lent a discrepant melancholy to his years.

Motionless on his mount, Abel watched as threads of white light entered in a spray from a low-lying bundle of clouds. A welcome, subtle peace slowly pervaded him as he relinquished the last, stubborn traces of duty's drudge. This day was his to live and explore as he chose.

"You ever see such a spectacular sunrise, Artemis?" Abel reached down and affectionately patted the moon-colored mare he had cared for since she was a filly four years earlier. Artemis' name had been inspired by a character from a favorite mythological story Abel's father had told him as a youngster. The name so perfectly suited her: Artemis—goddess of the moon, wild animals, and hunting.

At the sound of Abel's voice, Artemis whinnied and shook her mane as if in agreement with his appreciation of the sunrise. She seemed content to be accompanying her master during his short, carefree days.

The morning air was cold, but by afternoon the day would be hot, and a dry wind would create wind devils of gray dust. Abel twisted around in his saddle to catch sight of his well-packed gear and patted down his tight roll of blankets just behind him, instinctively double-checking the extra covers he had brought along. He had come prepared for more of the rare bracing cold that chilled the last couple of nights.

Abel knew most of the surrounding land well, and, for now, his two canvas canteens were full, giving him about two gallons for his immediate ride ahead. From the fort, he carried more than enough food in his saddlebags to last his trek.

Even so, small game was plentiful on the plains, and Abel was an experienced hunter.

Presently, Abel nudged his horse into a canter down the slope of the ridge toward the plain below. This day's journey, he had decided, would take him northeast toward an area he had not explored before. As he rode on, his thoughts again returned to the past: his father, Elijah, had been a just and good man who could stand up against aggression, but love was what he taught Abel most about.

Abel had witnessed the way Elijah cared deeply for Dancing Star, Abel's mother, and after she was killed, how he struggled to avoid vengeful bitterness. He saw how his father found the strength mostly to succeed in that, in his love for Abel and his father-in-law, Laughing Thunder. Of course, his love could not shield Abel from all the pain that was to come, but it did widen with understanding a young heart that might have been choked off with hate.

With the flow of memories, a gratifying thought struck Abel. The years of warring between two peoples had yielded to a temporary, local truce because of the love that joined together the hearts of his parents. During that love-induced truce, Abel had been born and raised for the first eight years of his life. Was that the faded remnant of a thought his father had left him or was it his own? No matter. It was a good feeling to think of himself as someone whole and nobly fashioned rather than as one who could not find himself in the pieces left to him.

8

CHAPTER THREE

As Elijah had told his son, Abel's grandfather was a Methodist preacher from Ohio who met and married a nurse in New York, where Elijah was born in 1812, the same year the English attacked the colonies but were rebuffed. After Elijah had earned his license to be a schoolteacher in New York, he taught for three years. He was twenty-four before the confining nature of his profession in a small town upstate grew too much for him. Abel knew he had been resolute when, in 1836, his sandy-haired, six-foot-tall father struck out by himself toward a new life with little more than his strong back and arms and an amiable disposition for the way. With God as his great companion, he headed west through the burgeoning town of St. Louis; camped a few days at Fort Laramie, an entry to the Rocky Mountains; and rode on into the Bitterroot Mountains of present Montana.

He camped in 1838 near a Nez Perce encampment in the future state of Washington. The friendly Nez Perce welcomed him, as they had welcomed quite a few immigrants and hunters before him, and taught him how to hunt and trap and live off the land. He discovered, quite happily, that he had found a new home.

Elijah mingled little with the other mountain men. Their rustic and often raucous lifestyles commonly led to drunkenness and fighting among themselves and neighboring Indian

9

traders. Abel deduced that his father, in contrast, was rare among the raw, semi-civilized mountain men. He was educated, pacific, and cultured, and he lived many of the Christian teachings of his minister father. Perhaps the most important characteristic in his new home in the Far West was his willingness to accept the Indians on their terms, yet contribute some of his useful Anglo traits, knowledge, and experience, as well.

In accord, however, with the other mountain men, Elijah was nourished by the grandeur of nature that surrounded him. Initially, he lacked very little either in physical or emotional needs amidst that time of contentment spent hunting, trading, and exchanging stories in the Indian camps. "But God, by way of life, leads you from one place to the next," Elijah would repeat to Abel more than once.

Just so, during a visit to the Nez Perce camp, Elijah met Dancing Star, a lovely and wise young woman of eighteen years. Petite, with flawlessly smooth, mahogany-brown skin, she had captivated twenty-six-year-old Elijah with her warm, black eyes, gentle smile, and loving disposition.

Dancing Star was the daughter of Laughing Thunder, the widowed Nez Perce chief with whom Elijah had developed a close friendship. Having a healthy and resonant sense of humor, Laughing Thunder's name fit well. He was not only the chief but the tallest man in his camp, meeting Elijah almost eye to eye at just over five feet, eleven inches tall. Then, thirty-eight years old and well-muscled at 170 pounds, the chief wore his straight, black hair in two thin braids descending to his chest but loosely and abundant in the back. A two-inch patch of thick hair stood up across his hairline at the top of his forehead, curving to one side in a somewhat feather fashion, which gave him, and many other Nez Perce chiefs, a unique and distinguished look.

Laughing Thunder's most winning characteristic, Elijah related to his son, was his natural leadership, for it bred a tranquil and friendly atmosphere among the Indians in the encampment.

Elijah often traded at the camp of Laughing Thunder, and, once he had met Dancing Star, he courted her at each of these opportunities. Through their lively exchanges of culture and language, a bond of mutual enjoyment grew between the two. It was clear to Abel when his father would recount the story, that from the first, Dancing Star was attracted to Elijah's easy, good-hearted manner and that, soon, she was as taken with him as he with her.

CHAPTER FOUR

According to Abel's father, the courtship of Abel's parents was unlike the casual agreements between an Indian family and the mountain men who selected Indian brides. At the Green River Rendezvous, held annually in the western region between the Green River and the Wind River Mountain Range, goods were given in exchange for wives during these carousing, days-long trade-offs between the Indians and the white hunters. The last Rendezvous was held in July of 1840. This Rendezvous Elijah attended, having been invited by Laughing Thunder, with Dancing Star wishing to accompany them both and after having gained her father's permission.

The gathering was also joined by the Belgian Jesuit missionary, Father Pierre-Jean De Smet, and the young Flathead Indian, Petit Ignace, who had guided the missionary there. De Smet's guide had been leading him on the way to start a mission among the groups of Flathead and Nez Perce Indians who had long requested and awaited a "Blackrobe's" arrival among them in their western lands of Montana. De Smet was well-known for his sincere peace efforts between the U. S. Army and various tribes of the northwest. He had gained a reputation for being just, fair, and kind among the Indians with whom he had arbitrated and those to whom he had introduced the Catholic faith. He was a man of deep conviction and

12

integrity and often disappointed by the Army's lack of integrity with the native tribes.

Although the missionary's popularity in the region was increasing quickly, none at this Green River gathering had personally met him. So it happened that, being greatly impressed with Father De Smet, and having discussed what was already so evident in their hearts, Dancing Star and Elijah asked that he baptize them, then perform their marriage at the Mass (the first Mass ever celebrated within today's boundaries of Wyoming) he was preparing at Green River that July 5, 1840. This became a special date that Abel would try to commemorate as he grew into adulthood.

By early August, Elijah and Dancing Star learned of a recently vacated farmhouse near Fort Walla Walla from one of their Nez Perce friends who knew of the couple's search for a place to build a homestead. The farm had been well-kept by the former occupants, who had decided to move to the newly developing farmlands in the Willamette Valley of western Oregon. Consequently, only a few repairs were needed. The minor mending and decorating needed was a job that both Elijah and Dancing Star greatly enjoyed, as together, they set up a home for themselves and the baby that was on the way.

The Wheatons had bartered with farming neighbors, as well as with friends they had cultivated in nearby tribes, to obtain seeds for various crops and small livestock, including six chickens and a rooster, a dozen sheep, four pigs, and a mating pair of goats. A few months later, they had bartered for a milk cow, three heifers, and a bull. This good business practice resulted in a flourishing beginning for their farm.

Often, after eating their afternoon meal during the long, warm evenings of August and September in that first year of their wedded life, Elijah spent his time carving out, sanding, and polishing a beautiful cradle of sturdy oak wood, while Dancing Star sat weaving a woolen baby blanket out of variously dyed threads she had made by hand and sewing baby clothes. When they were not speaking together of some news from the surrounding area, or planning for the months ahead, or just delighting in a topic of mutual interest, Dancing Star filled the night air with Nez Perce lullabies she hummed and sang to the little one within.

Seldom, too, especially as colder weather and early nightfall ushered the two indoors, did that mother's tender love omit reciting the Rosary prayers written down by Father De Smet and now memorized by her. Dancing Star's chain of *Hail Marys* was a gentle, echo-like chant as she thoughtfully passed her fingers over each polished agate bead of the rosary given to her and Elijah on their wedding day by the Jesuit missionary. Learning and reciting the Rosary was, however, a decidedly tedious chore for Elijah, who opted to tend to household tasks during its recitations, but who, nevertheless, found most pleasing the serenity that invariably enfolded him when, at his task, he united

14

inwardly to the unbroken murmur of prayers his wife sent softly upward.

Then, on the morning of April 16, 1841, as if on cue and in exuberant answer to those prayers, Abel Elijah Wheaton arrived at the homestead under a windswept, brilliant blue sky. At about eight pounds, and with all his toes and fingers, he was a healthy baby, with well-developed lungs to express both his desires and his discontents. Life for the young family all at once became more active and more challenging.

CHAPTER FIVE

That October, Elijah and his family traveled eastward to St. Mary's Mission, in the eastern part of Montana Territory. The mission had been founded under the leadership of Father De Smet and Abel was to be baptized there. This was a trip of about 375 miles from the farm, and partly in December, across the Bitterroot Mountains, where just thirty years earlier, the Lewis and Clark Expedition foundered in their winter-time crossing of that mountain mass and would have died without substantial help from the Nez Perce. Fortunately for Elijah and his family, they joined a band of thirty Nez Perce men led by Laughing Thunder, who knew the route well.

Laughing Thunder had been informed by a Flathead messenger that a large baptism ceremony was to take place at St. Mary's on Christmas Day that year and had passed the message on to his daughter and son-in-law, knowing that it was in their hearts to baptize Abel at the first opportunity. What was more, Laughing Thunder, too, desired baptism and had gathered the men of his clan who were of like mind to accompany him on the special journey. He had decided on a well-trusted brave of the tribe to take charge of the community's needs for the space of time he anticipated he would be away, about four

16

months, depending on weather conditions and any unforeseen circumstances that might occur.

Meanwhile, Elijah had requested at the nearby fort for an emigrant couple or family to stay on at the farm during the Wheatons' sojourn. That request was answered in short order when a family of four, one a newborn, welcomed the opportune break in their hard trek across the country so that the mother and newborn would be well-strengthened for the rest of the family's journey west into the Oregon Territory. The husband and father of that emigrant family and teenage son had been more than willing to look after the animals and upkeep of the farm, while the new mother recuperated and saw to the growing infant's needs as well as the household chores. In exchange for taking care of the Wheaton property and livestock, the emigrant family would receive free room and board, including free access to the eggs and dairy products acquired from the livestock, and to available crop vegetables, as well as having the right to any payment received from the sales of goods resulting from the family's work on the farm. The emigrant family was reported in very good standing by all the wagon train families who accompanied them, whom Elijah thoroughly interviewed. Satisfied with the chosen family and having made all the arrangements for their departure, the Wheatons set out well-prepared.

Winter had come early upon the small band of travelers heading over the range, with one ruddy infant held close against his mother's breast. Hence, eight-month-old baby Abel was carried eastward over the Bitterroot Mountains on the first rugged journey of his young life. During the impressive baptismal ceremony at St. Mary's on Christmas Day, 1841, 150 Flathead, demonstrably very glad of Father De Smet and his colleagues' long-awaited presence and work among them, and the thirty Nez Perce who had journeyed to the mission were baptized. Already baptized with Dancing Star the previous year at the Green River Rendezvous, Elijah, his wife, and now Abel and Laughing Thunder, too, would be joined together in the Catholic faith.

CHAPTER SIX

After returning to their farm, Abel and his parents enjoyed a family life of relative peace and friendship with nearby Cayuse tribes and the soldiers and settlers at nearby Fort Walla Walla. They exchanged crops, furs, and beef for supplies at the post. Abel not only mingled with the children of in-transit emigrants at the fort after he was about four years old, but his parents and he often visited the main Indian village of the strong Cayuse leader, Peopeo Moxmox, or Yellow Bird, only a couple of miles east of their farm. Here, even though he had been relatively small, Abel remembered the tall and confident Cayuse chief who always met him with a smile and a smartly fashioned toy, usually of wood or clay. And, here, whenever he arrived, the village children would rush to take possession of their little visitor and whisk him off on some new make-believe adventure or instruct him in one of their games, while his parents traded items and conversed with Yellow Bird and some of the village families.

Occasionally, the Wheatons would stay to partake of a meal with the chief's family or other close friends in the village. Other times, Indians, farming neighbors, or military friends visited the Wheatons at their tiny home on the farm. Those early years were golden, and Abel flourished. But darkness lay ahead for the little family.

Abel had been too young to remember the exact day tragedy struck and his mother died. The bitter cold of it, though, was there like biting shards of chiseled ice that pierced his heart whenever the memory slipped in unannounced, or he dared to recall what he could of that day. The month was December of 1847. Dancing Star, Elijah, and Abel had gone into the trading post at Fort Walla Walla to buy supplies. They were unaware of the attack that had occurred shortly before, on November 29th, at the Whitman Mission, twenty-six miles east of the fort. Both the mission founder, Marcus Whitman, also a medical doctor, and his wife Narcissa had fallen victims to a small band of Cayuse Indians after repeated warnings from two of the more hostile Cayuse leaders to vacate the area.

The missionaries, boarders, and many emigrants who had stopped to rest at the mission on their way west had been killed, seriously wounded, or taken hostage. These Indians had grown more and more mistrustful of and combative against white intruders. Finally, when a measles epidemic spread from a group of settlers to the Cayuse, who had no resistance to the disease, half of the tribe was wiped out despite Dr. Whitman's best efforts to cure them. When the Indians saw that the white children were revived by Whitman's medicine but not any of their own, they concluded that Whitman had poisoned them. To retaliate, they went on a rampage.

Few had escaped, but one of the emigrants who had seen his wife brutally murdered managed to flee. Although wounded, he hiked by foot westward along the northern bank of the Walla Walla River, crossed the Touchet River where it joined with the Walla Walla, and crossed the plain to the fort. When he arrived, he was still bleeding from a head wound and several knife wounds. Helped through the gate of the fort by a well-meaning sentry, the emigrant, half-crazed and exhausted, saw in front of him a soldier conversing with Elijah and Dancing Star.

Infuriated by the sight of this Indian woman, he wrested the soldier's gun from him and fired. Dancing Star died quickly in the arms of her husband and son. The man, still screaming accusations of savages, then turned the gun on himself. Later, Elijah would learn the details of the massacre and would explain to his son, as well as he could, the tragedy at the mission that led to his innocent mother's death.

As Dancing Star was the daughter of one of the Nez Perce leaders, the Nez Perce in general, and her friends in particular, were greatly saddened by her untimely and violent death. They began a traditional mourning period of five days during which she was ritually bathed, combed and her face decorated with red paint. She was dressed in her finest clothes, including a white deerskin dress, simply fringed at the collar and the mid-calf hemline with leather cords of yellow and blue beads. Then she was wrapped in a beige wool blanket, woven in the

21

center with a pink sun-like pattern. A medicinal bundle was folded into the blanket, along with her most valuable possessions, including her wedding band, the fine woolen baby blanket lovingly woven with hand-dyed strands of delicate blues and greens in which she had wrapped Abel for the first six months of his life.

Fortuitously, one of Father De Smet's priests had arrived at Fort Walla Walla on a visit through the region both to proselytize the un-baptized Indians and to teach and encourage "the faithful." At Elijah's request, the priest willingly celebrated a final Mass with everyone present before Dancing Star was buried.

A wooden cross, beautifully carved and inscribed by Laughing Thunder as a last gift to his daughter, was set as a marker for her on a 250-foot-high bluff overlooking the Nez Perce encampment. In that way, both her Indian origins and family and her Catholic faith and faithfulness were honored.

As the mourning continued, however, another Nez Perce tradition was followed faithfully: her name was not spoken again by the Nez Perce, although she could be remembered in discussions by referring to her using another title. The Nez Perce believed this practice allowed her to enter the spirit world unhindered. The title chosen for Dancing Star by her father, Laughing Thunder, was "Woman of Two Nations."

Elijah, Abel, and the Catholic priest, of course, anticipated that this good Indian woman, wife of a good, moral Anglo man, and

22

mother of a good, moral son of mixed Indian/Anglo blood was on her way to heaven. Given her exemplary life, who would contest that?

Grief-stricken after the death of Dancing Star, Elijah did not want to stay at the home the two of them had built together, but the winter of 1847-1848 was so harsh that Elijah and Abel had to postpone their departure until the spring of 1848.

As soon as the weather permitted, Elijah traveled south with his son and settled on another farm, this time near a Hudson's Bay Co. trading post called Fort Boise, built in 1834, at the confluence of the Boise River with the Snake River.

The new farm was similar in size to the first but with added grazing acreage for the two milk cows and a dozen cattle, sheep, and goats. But the house itself was smaller and did not have the fine touches that only a woman's presence could have provided. Abel's time at this farm, however, would be short once more because, as for so many other settlers, he and his father would be engaged again by one of the many calamities that harassed both the settlers and the Indians in this wild country about 1500 miles west of the Mississippi River and St. Louis.

CHAPTER SEVEN

One of Abel's happiest recollections was the story his mother told him about the origin of his name, decided on before his birth. She had been hoping for a boy and wanted to name him Abel, after the Bible's first shepherd boy, whose offerings were so pleasing to God. The simple story of the shepherd's earnest love for his Creator, which contrasted so sharply with the envious hatred of his brother, Cain, held an unexpected appeal for Dancing Star. Aside from the much longer Nativity narrative, which mesmerized his bright, young wife most of all, Elijah was repeatedly called upon by Dancing Star to retell the much shorter Bible story concerning young Abel and his honest, humble friendship with God. Although its ending always brought tears, it was, however, especially for Cain, that Dancing Star shed the most poignant tears of sorrow because of his obstinate blindness to the irreplaceable gifts of love that surrounded him. Cain's brother Abel, in both life and death, brought her the joyful solace of having remained steadfastly with his God.

So it was that from his first breath, the baby had been dubbed Abel Elijah Wheaton. His parents hoped that he, too, would grow morally good, physically strong, and very pleasing

24

before the Great Spirit; but also that he would be kept in the mighty protection of his wise Creator all the days of his life.

So far, Abel mused wryly, that protection seemingly had been only intermittent. And yet, the thought stirred within him that something of significance and special purpose lay before him, even as he pressed on in bewilderment about what that might be.

Playing against his intuitive hope, a recent entanglement with emigrants at Fort Laramie last May had ignited stark images of the past. For several weeks, he had been able to subdue the onerous darkness of those oppressive memories. This last week, however, they had returned with a vengeance suffocating any brave efforts on Abel's part to dismiss them. One of those May afternoons at the fort rose up in his mind most vividly of all.

A seemingly drunk man lay in the street outside the supply store when Abel emerged from it that day. Another man approached and asked Abel for a hand in getting him up the street to a temporary bed in the doc's office. As Abel approached the prostrate man, the other butted him on the back of the head enough to daze him and grab the gun from his holster. One of the men put him into an arm-lock, while the other thug roughly gagged him, then both of the strangers forcibly escorted Abel and shoved him behind the blacksmith's shop. He was forced back to his feet and held in a tight grip, wrists jammed upwards against his back by the larger man. Then, having cruelly

25

brought the hot brand to Abel's eyes for examination, the shorter man whispered to Abel venom-filled words that crawled deep into his stomach. "No matter how civilized you may try to look and act, you'll always be a s-s-savage at heart to everybody else."

Abel was sickened as he desperately watched the man's burning eyes and wicked, half-turned smile, just behind the red embers drifting off the fire-hot "s." "And to remind you of it, we're leaving you with a little engraving—right above your heart."

Everything in the suffocating air surrounding Abel froze. Oddly, too, even the unbearable pain searing his chest burned with less intensity when he heard a rifle being cocked. The man behind him eased his grip on Abel's arms. The other man lost his wicked sneer and withdrew the hot brand while turning his head askance to check the source of the sudden sound.

"Drop it now, and let him go," a deep, forceful voice rang out. There, behind the young man's aggressor, stood Gabe, the Fort Laramie blacksmith, bigger and more welcome than any life-sized angel Abel could have wished for at that moment. Immediately, Abel was released as the two drunken torturers ran away, with the enormous Negro man still aiming his rifle at them.

Not bothering with a follow-up glance toward the fleeing figures, Gabriel lowered his weapon and moved quickly to Abel, who lay on the dirt ground behind the blacksmith's shop.

"Abe!" Gabriel laid down his rifle and lifted Abel's throbbing head to untie the gag that had been drawn oppressively taut between his jaws. "How'd you let yourself be put in such a situation, son? I know you got more brains than them two put together, and I'm certain you got more skill with a gun." The big man's reprimand held no trace of sympathy as he deftly worked to untie Abel, but his face was the purest compassion. "Where is your gun anyway, Abe?" Gabriel's eyes searched the surrounding dust. He spied it lying about three yards away, close to the dumpster in the alley beside the blacksmith's shop. With a lunge, Gabe speedily retrieved the revolver, then slipped and locked it back into its owner's holster.

Gabriel Foster, who had been born a free black in the East, had been Fort Laramie's blacksmith for about five years. Muscular from practicing his trade, he was a huge man who kept his head bald, his eyes alert, and a story to tell. Abel had met him several months before while enlisting with the Pony Express. Abel lived just outside Fort Laramie, and the two commonly had long, friendly talks whenever Abel visited to pick up supplies and later, whenever the two met after his mail runs were completed at the fort. But he had never been happier to see the burly giant of a man than that day.

Abel struggled to form a reply as he felt the rescuer's arms reach gently under him, but his jaws still felt wired shut, and his body was in

27

shock from fighting the pain the brand had inflicted.

"I'm taking you to the fort surgeon right now. You look terrible. Just you be quiet. We'll discuss this later," said Gabe.

Abel's futile attempts at explanation, his exhaustion and his pain had all been silenced for the moment as he lost consciousness. The last memory he had before waking in the surgeon's office was that of being lifted and carried like a babe down the dusty street in Gabe's arms.

Later that day, after the doctor had tended the burn so that Abel recuperated from the pain and regained a little animation, he recounted for Gabe and the doctor what had happened.

After Abel's attackers had been described to the doctor, the latter recognized them as men who had attached themselves to an emigrant party on their way to the Oregon country. An Indian band had converged on them about fifty miles east of Fort Laramie, took their livestock, and killed two of the men of the party.

Abel supposed he had been pointed out offhandedly as a half-blood to his assailants in the supply store where he remembered first seeing them. The phrase, "Injun pony rider," was spewed repeatedly in Abel's face, along with a profuse deriding of anything and anyone Indian. The offenders had either crudely made or, more likely, found at the blacksmith's shop an old branding iron with an "s"-shaped symbol, perfect for signifying the word "savage."

The burn from the red-hot branding iron eventually healed into a scar, but on certain days, Abel struggled against a mental pain worse than he suffered from the branding. Indeed, lately the saddest, most frightful moments of his childhood and young manhood played out, relentlessly it seemed, like scenes of an egregious drama before him as he speedily galloped, alone and unencumbered, along the Pony Express route.

CHAPTER EIGHT

When Abel set out from Fort Laramie the previous day, the burden he carried inside had grown to a heaviness greater than any material baggage he could have loaded upon Artemis for their stay in the wilderness. But now, he was calm and enjoying the early morning on the High Plains.

Having ridden several more miles northeast of his campsite last night, Abel gave a tug on his horse's reins and nudged her to an easy trot. First basking in the majesty of the outstretched plains, Abel then gazed ahead to see retreating antelope bounding away from him toward a small herd of buffalo feasting on the plains grass about a quarter-mile away to the west. The leader of the herd watched Abel and his horse warily for a minute, but he appeared to find no cause for alarm and returned to his feeding.

"What do you say, Artemis? How 'bout we camp on that isolated ridge we saw from our camp last night, girl?" said Abel, smoothing the horse's neck. Then squinting as he surveyed the blueness above him, he added, "Stars'll sure be bright. Sky's already crystal blue, and it'll be cloudless soon with this breeze."

Artemis neighed and tossed her head, shaking her white mane as if to interrupt Abel's report.

30

"What?" Abel gently stroked her once more. "Yes, I know there's been an unusual cold trend these last few nights. But don't worry, girl; I brought extra blankets." He laughed heartily and lovingly patted Artemis on the neck.

Suddenly Abel noticed a small figure in the distance and drew Artemis to a halt. He strained his eyes to see who was running toward him.

"Mister! Please wait!"

Abel had Artemis quicken her pace to meet the stranger who apparently needed help. There before him was a young black boy, about twelve years old. With spindly but strong-looking forearms lifting high out of the tattered sleeves of his dusty, blue shirt, the boy continued waving and crossing his hands in the air as he ran forward, calling to Abel. Close to him now, Abel searched the wide, pleading eyes and round, expressive face of the young stranger.

Abel watched with charmed curiosity as the boy's one dimple, planted deep in his left cheek, vanished and reappeared in rapid succession as he fired off a long string of words.

"Please, mister, my mama's gettin' worse. Please come help her. My brother's gone for medicine, but I don't know if he got lost. Jake's been gone awful long; Mama and me both agree he shouldn't be takin' this long. Trouble started when we all didn't know where we was, and Mama got awful tired. But we'll be all right now. It won't take long to get there; she's over this way," said the boy without drawing one new breath and already pulling at Artemis' harness to lead the horse and rider in the right direction.

"Whoa, there. Hold on," Abel said, tugging the reins gently to hold Artemis in place.

The boy stopped and turned. His disappointed eyes met Abel's. "Why? Ain't you gonna help?" he asked. "I knew when I started walking that I'd find someone. I prayed before I left her. Mama says prayers are answered. Some, not so quick. But I was lucky; I found you right away. Now you're gonna tell me you ain't gonna help?"

"No, young man, I didn't mean that." Abel tipped back his hat a bit and leaned down over the horn of his saddle toward the disgruntled lad still blocking the way, nor had he loosened his grip on the harness. "I was only trying to slow down your tongue." A smile crept across Abel's face and likewise invaded the boy's. "Of course, I'll see what I can do for your ma. You just lead the way." Then Abel reached down, offering a hand to his new companion. "But you can ride, you know. There's plenty room up here for both of us." And he pulled the boy up behind him.

"Gee, thanks, mister." The boy pointed northward. "Go that way," he said and off galloped Artemis.

"What's your name?" asked Abel.

"William Pearce; what's yours?"

"Just call me Abe; everyone else does."

"Okay, Abe. I like that name. Abe." William seemed to like the sound of it bouncing off his tongue as he gave it another try. "It's short for Abraham, ain't it? Mama told me all 'bout him, the Abraham in the Bible, I mean. He was the one God promised all the land and descendants to. One of the greatest men ever lived, Ma says, because his goodness and his faith in God was so powerful. Why even the next president is named after him."

"The next president?" Abel could not help turning in his saddle enough to give William a perplexing side-glance. "I admire your hope."

Shaking his head and dismissing William's remark, Abel straightened up and chuckled at the young man's lively love of conversation. "Sorry to disappoint you, William. I'm not named after the great Abraham. But my namesake is in the Bible, too. I'm Abel, like the shepherd of Cain and Abel fame."

With that, the boy's exuberance faded. "Oh," said William. "Well, I know 'bout him, too."

Abel raised a curious eyebrow at the short, silent interval that ensued, but William very soon re-focused his attention on a small grouping of rock formations peaking twenty feet or so above the plain's surface ahead of them. With revived animation, William bounced on his seat and pointed toward the largest rock. "Mama's just 'round that big rock there! She'll be mighty glad to see you, Abe; I know she will."

"Let's hope so, William. I'm sure the two of us working together can help your ma." Abel reassured his new young friend with a smile. "What does she go by?" Abel inquired.

"Grace is her name," said William.

CHAPTER NINE

Something about William disturbed Abel when he first drew the boy up behind him onto Artemis, but he had no time to ponder it because the boy continued to chatter incessantly. Now it crystallized as Abel looked down at William's thin arms casually wrapped around his own waist. As one of the boy's dark, slender arms was now bared against the blue cotton fabric of an upturned sleeve, Abel could see whip scars sliced across his skin. A horrifying chill crawled over him as he stared at the looming rock just ahead. His mind shot back five years to 1855, to the bitterness of a life-changing day for him when he was fourteen years old.

Elijah and Abel had lived peacefully on the second farm for seven years. Father and son had struggled to get beyond their grief, but to Abel, that had seemed more difficult for his father. Elijah had been a strong man in many ways, but Abel grew to most admire his will to love, to remain a God-fearing man in spite of circumstances. He was in awe of the power this gave Elijah to get on with life when others succumbed to their grief. And, of course, the hard work of the farm, as well as the pleasure of the fishing and the hunting, had been palliatives that helped ease his grief as time went by. Still, Dancing Star was never far from the thoughts of the father and the son.

Abel and his father had often visited the boy's grandfather, Laughing Thunder, and the Nez Perce people to the north. Abel knew from listening to their conversations that the promises of the white man were not being honored, and the long-standing peace between his mother's people and the new government, which intruded upon their way of life, was strained dangerously.

Although only six years old when his mother had died, Abel remembered that both the grief and consolation had been shared by Laughing Thunder and Elijah over the loss of Dancing Star. They needed each other, no matter how different they were, in order to heal and become whole again. Abel had also observed as time passed that he, in some strange way, was the new light in which they placed their future hopes. Abel had been too young to form it in words, but the light was there between the two men, nevertheless, and he knew.

The occasions that brought his father and grandfather together inspired Abel to expand his own horizons. When they visited the tribe, Abel would learn traditions of the Nez Perce that recalled to him special times spent with his mother and the lessons she had taught him, though some had slipped away. He enjoyed the company of others his age who taught him new ways to look at life; they taught him practical skills with a knife and bow and arrow, not to mention the fine art of carving lovely wood sculptures that his grandfather had practiced with him; and his father continued to teach him the skills of farming and ranching, as well as of a handgun, rifle, and knife, and the skills of hunting well beyond his years. The tribe's natural sharing and mutual concern for each other brought warmth to Abel's lonely heart, a heart that had always been torn with sadness whenever he and his father departed for home.

On a day almost eight years after his mother's death, Abel's life would be seriously disrupted with renewed grief as grave calamity struck again. As with the Cayuse at Walla Walla, the Shoshoni in that part of the country where the Wheatons farmed, had watched the waves of white settlers arrive, who, supported by their government, had seemed determined to claim all the land for themselves.

In the early morning of April 20, 1855, a large band of Shoshoni had attacked a wagon train of emigrants about to arrive at Fort Boise. A handful of infantry soldiers were sent out to the Wheaton farm to provide protection, but three Shoshoni braves already were riding up to the farmhouse. Elijah and his son, who were just getting ready to clear the breakfast table, had heard the horses approach the house, then a voice demanding that the house's occupants come out.

"It's the Shoshoni, Abe." Elijah rose from the sand-polished, rough-hewn table and reached for his rifle, which was standing against the ash-filled hearth. "Your grandfather and I felt something was coming, just not this soon. Still, I should have left you with him for a while, like he offered." Elijah slid a pistol across the table to his son. "Take this, Abe; it's loaded. Let's hope they're not at war with the whites...or us."

Abel had watched his father's face with silent worry as Elijah nodded toward the weapon he had given his son. "Don't hesitate a moment to use it, if the need comes, Abel. Do you understand, son?" His father's serious tone had demanded acknowledgment, and Abel gave it, despite the growing sick feeling of fear wanting to surface in some awkward display of emotion.

But Abel had remained quiet and alert as Elijah marched toward the four-paned, draped window to the left of the front door in the small, plank-wood cabin. Elijah had motioned for Abel to get low and to move to the rear of the room. Taking the revolver with him, Abel quickly followed his father's instructions, positioning himself on one knee below a smaller back window of the cabin. Then, with caution, Elijah slightly drew back one blue gingham curtain panel to get a glimpse of the uninvited visitors, who by the sound of their voices and their horses' hooves were just a few yards in front of the house.

Three mounted Shoshoni, each with an arrow fixed in his bow, pointed toward the cabin door. On seeing Elijah's face appear in the corner of the window, the Shoshoni leader gave up a yell, and all three arrows whirred and hit the door.

"Get down, Abe!" shouted Elijah as he broke the left bottom pane of the window with the butt of his rifle and fired a single shot at one of the two dismounted and advancing Indians. That Indian fell over backwards and lay dead about six feet from the porch, but the second Indian on foot had vanished from the front of the house and had raced around to the back of the cabin. Abel heard a hard thud on the back door as the Indian tried to force his way in; fortunately, the door was securely barred with a six-by-four wood beam.

Meanwhile, the lead Indian, who had remained on his mount, had lighted a torch of dry sticks tied into a bunch and quickly threw it on top of the cabin's thickly thatched roof. Elijah returned to the window, aimed and fired at the mounted Indian. The rifle bullet hit the Indian in the chest and catapulted him backward off his horse. He dropped to the ground like a limp bundle, undoubtedly dead. His horse cantered away.

Only one of the three Shoshoni attackers remained alive, but smoke now filled the cabin as the fire on the roof had spread quickly, and a burning ceiling log threatened to collapse into the room and bring a large part of the roof with it. Suddenly the sound of shattering glass came from the window above Abel. The last remaining Indian, now still outside but at the back of the farmhouse, had yanked the hanging curtain from its thin rod and peered inside the room. The opening was too small for even a slight man to be able to crawl through without great difficulty, let alone the muscular brave who was still stalking Elijah and Abel.

Before the Indian could get his arm completely out, Abel, kneeling below the window, fired his revolver. The bullet creased the Indian's arm, causing him to yelp in pain and race away from the window.

Elijah shouted, "We must run for it, Abe!" Abel shot to his side, and Elijah drew him quickly near, gripping his son's shoulder. Abel's father had lowered the heavy beam from the back door. Elijah then opened the door an inch or so to look out, then pointed about twenty-five yards away to an old oak tree on the property. Hoping that the oak's trunk, a good six feet in diameter, would provide some cover, he pointed to the tree and quietly ordered Abel, "Run behind that oak! I'm right behind you, son!"

Abel made it to the tree well before his father.

Elijah rapidly followed behind, his rifle swinging from side to side. Their tiny home was now well engulfed in flames.

Suddenly, Abel watched as Elijah fell to his knees, an arrow in his back. Rage filled Abel.

The attacker threw his bow and empty quiver abruptly to the ground and quickly snatched a whip from his horse to aid him in a swift and sure attack if his prey were to anticipate him and try to flee. Abel watched, hidden, and strangely self-possessed by the fury he felt against the Indian who had killed his father and who now prevented him from reaching his father's side. The Shoshoni unfurled the whip and, with deadly malice, snapped it twice as he approached the oak tree.

With a knife in the other hand, the Indian was ready to strike the boy, whom he surely did not fear. But Abel quickly stepped around the tree

39

before the warrior could wield the whip, charge, or dodge. He fired two shots in succession. Both bullets hit the Indian in the chest and killed him instantly.

Although now small comfort to Abel, that ended the fight at the farm. Abel then raced to help Elijah, but it was too late. The Indian warrior, an experienced fighter in many skirmishes and wars with other tribes, had shot his arrow fast and true; and Elijah, only forty-three years old, widower, father, farmer, hunter, had lived only a few moments more. Sobbing, Abel had pressed his tear-stained cheek against his father's still face. Both of his parents, now murdered and lost forever to him in this life, Abel, only fourteen years old, felt an unbridled desolation, with hope lost. God seemed to have abandoned him.

Within minutes after this battle ended, five troopers from the fort had arrived. Having heard their approach, Abel reached into his father's right trouser pocket, and he withdrew an object concealed in his fist. He held it a moment before plunging it into his own pocket and fell once more against the still-warm, lifeless body of his father, to which he clung until a soldier coaxingly pulled him to his feet.

The soldiers searched the area for other Indians who might have been hiding. Finding none, they hurriedly used their trenching tools to dig a deep grave under the long branches of the oak tree, buried Elijah in it, and placed a wooden cross at the head of the grave, with

"Elijah" scratched on the cross arm. With Abel in tow, they returned to the fort, where he would be safe from other bands of marauding Indians who might come to the farm searching for their three companions.

A few days later, the soldiers and Abel, who was still in shock, had returned to the farm to bring the livestock to the fort, where it was sold to emigrants who stayed overnight there. That provided Abel with a small amount of "seed money" to help him begin his premature entry into adult life. His father's parents, whom he had never met, and who knew nothing of Abel, their grandson, lived in the state of New York, a world away. His Nez Perce grandfather, who almost certainly had not heard yet about the death of his son-in-law, or the orphanhood of his grandson, Abel, was probably with a hunting party in the Bitterroot Valley, about 250 miles away to the east.

At that moment, Abel truly had felt alone and on his own...except for the kindness and generosity of the soldiers and their families at the fort. But that "spring of goodness" likely would soon run dry as new, equally demanding problems developed for the families.

Abel became a ward of the U. S. Army for only a short time at Fort Boise. When word of his son-in-law's death had reached Laughing Thunder the following month, he came immediately to the fort and claimed Abel as the boy's remaining relative.

For reasons unknown to Abel, Elijah had broken all ties with his family in the East before his son had been born, and that family was little spoken of except in short comments in answer to Abel's questions. Abel wondered as time passed, however, if Elijah's Protestant parents, his father a minister, would have accepted, without acrimony or anger, either Elijah's marriage to "a heathen Indian woman" or his transformation to Catholicism.

The commandant of the fort had no qualms about allowing the half-breed Abel to return to "Indian country" with his grandfather. As Laughing Thunder, a childless widower, delighted in Abel's company, grandfather and grandson had lived together in the Nez Perce village for the next two years in a harmony that helped to ease Abel's loss.

CHAPTER TEN

With the discovery of William's whip marks, Abel rightly reasoned that the boy and his family must, at some point, have been living as slaves, but he resolved to let their story unfold as they desired to reveal it. His only two considerations right now were to discover the seriousness of Grace's condition to offer what help he could and to alleviate the anxiety of his new, lively, young acquaintance.

Abel and William did not have far to ride to the campsite. Its thick grass reached the apparent boundary of the almost barren, sandy ground where the Pearce family had set up camp in the shelter of the large sandstone outcrop.

William's mother lay on a bedroll with a colorful but worn handmade quilt covering her. Abel dismounted several yards from Grace's bed and tethered Artemis to the low branch of a small tree. The horse began to nibble the abundant grass from a large patch of green meadow.

Abel crouched down beside the woman. Only her head was visible, and her rich, brown skin tone was a shade darker than William's. She seemed to be soundly asleep. He felt her forehead and cheeks and noted, with relief, no evidence of smallpox, the scourge of the region. He looked across at William, who had bent down on the other side of his mother. "Your ma has a fever, William, but it's not high yet. Do you think you can tell me slowly and briefly what happened? When did she start feeling poorly?"

"Her head was hurtin' some, and she said she couldn't breathe so good. Is she gonna be okay?"

After a brief examination, Abel was certain he could help William's mother. "I think your ma has an illness that can become very serious if not treated."

William's eyes widened.

"I know about some plants that yield a medicine that should help her to fight the sickness."

William scrunched his nose and eyebrows at the word "yield" but seemed to understand the general idea.

Abel continued, "They commonly grow by streams crossing the plains here." Abel leaned across the sleeping Grace and put his hand on William's shoulder. "I promise not to leave you until your brother gets back. Now, can you tell me how long ago he left?"

"Jake left yesterday mornin'. Mama was too weak and tired to keep on travelin'."

"He didn't go on foot, did he?"

William shook his head. "Took our only horse; Indians stole our other one. Took his canteen of water, some dishes, the rifle and his bedroll, that's all. He left us with the rest of these here supplies." William motioned toward a few bundles, a small bedroll, two canteens, two sets of clean tin cups and platters with forks, and a medium-size iron pot lying next to a nearby

44

campfire site. "Said he'd be back 'fore long. He rode out that way." William pointed west.

Abel sighed and bowed his head. "Nothing out that way for miles." He glanced at William. "So he'll probably be returning soon anyway because he won't find anything, except maybe Indians, and they may not take kindly to him. Anyway, he'll be worried about you two." Then, motioning to William, he rose. "You stay here by your ma; I'll be right back."

As Abel turned to go, William's mother, in an assertive but raspy voice, broke in. "Who's that you're talkin' to, William?" She had awakened and was lifting herself on her elbows.

William stepped up. "This is Abe, Mama; that's short for Abel. He's gonna make you well again, so soon as Jake comes, we can leave."

"Oh, he is, is he?" Briefly eyeing the newcomer, she looked again at William and drew a breath. "Did you go wanderin' off after I told you to stay put?"

"I knew I wouldn't have to go far, Mama. I wasn't walkin' an hour when I spotted Abe, here, ridin' my way."

The woman squinted into Abel's face and struggled to speak. "You mean to tell me, my William..." She coughed. "Simply ran up to you." She paused as if to gain strength to speak. "And laid hold of your horse's reins, then pulled you here, and you, givin' no objections?"

Abel's eyebrows shot up as he gave a swift nod and smiled. "That's about the size of it, ma'am."

45

"Well, bless the good Lord's name. You must be 'bout as lightheaded as my own boy, here." They both laughed.

"Could be, ma'am, but he did seem distressed, and I couldn't very well run him over where he stood."

The woman's smile was radiant, despite her sickness. "I reckon not," she said. "Abe, for short, is it?"

He nodded.

"I'm Grace," she said, offering her hand.

"Pleased to meet you, Grace," Abel returned, stooping down low again and gently shaking her hand.

Although Grace was not standing, Abel could see that she was a small-framed woman of average height. She appeared about fifty, give or take a year, and wore her coarse, graying hair pulled up and wound into a thick, braided bun that sat almost on the top of her head, affording her more comfort, Abel imagined, when she slept. The light cotton dress she wore was olive green with long sleeves, one frayed and torn a bit at the top right shoulder, and with a scooped plain white collar close to the neck. In facial appearance, the resemblance between her and William was uncanny, save for the fact that Grace possessed not just one elusive dimple, as William did, but one planted in each cheek of her round face, and which Abel had immediately observed when she first had begun speaking.

"My other son will be returnin' soon, so there's no need to keep you," Grace continued politely. "I do thank you, though, for bein' kind enough to...."

"I know, Grace," Abel cut in. "William filled me in on some of the details, and I've decided to stay until your son returns."

Grace opened her mouth to object, but Abel persisted.

"No, ma'am; no 'buts'; and to be honest, you do need tending to, and I think I can help."

"An angel outta the middle of nowhere," said Grace half aloud and then lay back down again, her eyes wandering back to William with a wink.

William smiled and winked back.

"You won't see a halo on me, Grace." Abel's face suddenly felt warm. "But this plain ol' fella thinks he can help you get well again."

"Ain't many'd do that much if it'd take 'em outta their way. You're an angel, all right." Grace paused. "I know Jake'll be returnin' soon, but the truth is, I am feelin' weak and a bit shaky." She shivered as she drew up her quilt under her chin. "Wish we had more blankets. It's sure gettin' chilly."

"But, Mama, it ain't cold." William's expression grew serious.

Abel touched her face again and turned a sober look toward the boy.

"The fever's gone up, William. How much water's in your canteens?" Abel nodded toward the containers.

"One of 'em's full." William immediately brought the canteen to Abel, who unscrewed its top, poured some of the water into one of the tin

47

cups next to the campfire site, and lifted Grace's head.

"When's the last time you drank anything, Grace?" asked Abel.

She answered slowly. "Just before I drifted off to sleep again this mornin'. Jake found a creek right near here, and he filled up two canteens before he left."

"You're going to need to drink more."

Grace nodded as Abel took charge.

"Your fever'll be getting worse, I'm afraid. The couple of extra blankets I brought with me should help to keep you as comfortable as possible." Abel faced William. "Bring me one of the smaller blankets strapped to the back of the saddle on my horse, will you, William?"

"Right," returned William; he dashed the twenty or so yards to get to Artemis. Then William pulled himself up onto the saddle where he could readily reach the blankets. He unfastened the tight roll of one thick and two thin wool blankets, chose one of the smaller ones, and bunched it under one arm, then quickly re-rolled the other two and hugged the roll under his other arm before he nimbly jumped down from the horse and ran back to Abel. William held out the bunched blanket to Abel and let the roll he toted drop to the ground. "Brought them all just in case."

"Good thinking, William." Abel grinned at the earnest, good-natured boy and then spread the blanket over Grace.

He looked again at William. "You stay here with your ma. Give her as much water as she'll

48

take, and see if you can build up a fire in the campfire pit. I'll be right back. Oh, and tell me, which way is the creek you found?"

"No more'n five minutes that way." William pointed with a stick to the north.

Abel grabbed the strap of the almost empty canteen and slung it on his shoulder.

"Why? Gonna get more water?"

"That's right. And something else that'll help your ma—ingredients for an old Indian recipe." Abel headed toward Artemis. He approached the horse, opened the saddlebag, pulled out a red apple, and held it to Artemis' mouth; she crunched off half of it and chomped it down; in another bite, she polished off the rest. "Sweet and juicy, eh girl?" Abel's tone soothed her, and he affectionately stroked Artemis' silver-gray coat under her jaw with his left hand and smoothed her long, white forehead and nose. Then he stepped to Artemis' side, caught the saddle horn, and easily hoisted himself up. After hooking William's canteen strap over the saddle horn with his own, Abel softly clucked to Artemis and tugged the reins to veer her in the direction of the creek. "C'mon, girl; let's get you some nice fresh water to wash down that snack." He patted Artemis' neck, then rode away from the camp, past another massive rock outcrop.

***

William got the fire started shortly thereafter by using a mixture of wood and some of the buffalo chips he had gathered from the surrounding shortgrass prairie the day before

49

and was helping his mother to a second drink from the tin cup Abel had filled for her when something caught his attention.

"Look, Ma!" William pointed up the side of the rocky outcrop by the campsite as an orange-tan-and-black-colored horned lizard scurried over the top and, apparently, down the other side of the rock. "There goes one of them spiky critters I seen yesterday! I'm gonna catch him so we can get a good look at him. I gotta show Abe. Be right back, Ma."

"William, don't you be wanderin' off like you did last time, you hear me?" cautioned his mother.

***

In a short time, however, Abel was back and dismounted Artemis, this time removing his saddle and gear and placing them on the ground close to his horse. With a large handful of twigs and small leafy plants, he approached Grace, who was resting but awake. "Where's William?" he asked, scanning the area for the missing lad.

"Went after one of them 'spiky critters' he calls 'em. Says he's gonna fetch it for us to see." Grace smiled.

"Oh, he must have found a horned lizard; most folks call them 'horny toads' because of their round bellies," Abel replied, returning Grace's smile. "Interesting little guys, especially for a boy who's not used to seeing them."

***

Grace watched as Abel proceeded to place more wood on the campfire. The crackling of

50

the new wood burning, the red embers dusting the air, and the pleasant smoky aroma wafting about the fire warmed and comforted Grace. Abel, engaged in his task, ground the twigs and plants between two stones into small pieces and carefully added them to the water in one of the canteens. After shaking the canteen well, Abel poured its contents into the clean pot beside him, hung the pot from a sturdy stick bridge, probably built by Jake, over the fire pit, and allowed the mixture to heat until it boiled slowly for several minutes.

Abel walked to where he had set his saddle and gear on the ground close to Artemis. He crouched down to unstrap from his pack the light wool coat he had brought for riding under the stars in case of more unseasonably cold nights. Then he sat on the ground beside Artemis but facing away from Grace.

Artemis whinnied softly and gently tossed her mane as if in question. "Don't worry, girl; nothing to worry about," he said in a calming voice as he reached out to gently stroke and pat her foreleg nearest to him. Then he drew a light-green bandana from his trouser pocket, spread it on the dirt next to him, and, pulling a knife from its scabbard strapped onto the outer side of his right boot, he began to cut and tear strips from the coat's cotton lining.

Grace's eyes widened. "Abe, that's your coat! What're you doin', son?" She tried to sit up, almost frantic. She had curiously eyed his movements since he walked away and plainly distinguished the ripping sounds now.

51

***

"You need it right now more than I do. Just settle down, Grace. Everything's all right." Abel tried to calm her as she leaned on an elbow and continued to watch him with apprehension until he had completed his task of collecting several strips of lining from the lower half of the coat and placing them one at a time on top of the bandana in a growing heap. Then tying the bandana corners together over the cloth strips with one, quick pull, he put his knife back, re-strapped the coat to his pack, and returned with his bundle to Grace's side. He leaned over to check the nearby bubbling water in the pot and removed it from the fire, well away from Grace. Sitting down beside her, Abel nodded cheerfully to Grace and placed the bundle next to him. He then untied and opened the bandana, ready to separate the cloth strips from the semi-tangled clump.

Grace lay down again and sighed softly. "You're part Indian, ain't that right, Abe? It's noticeable. You have the handsome features of your people."

Abel lifted an eyebrow. The unexpected comment brought a flush of embarrassment to his face once more.

Clearly disregarding his reaction, Grace went on. "And your ma—bet she taught you 'bout— which plants—are good for this or that ailment."

Abel's clear, deep-set eyes became intently focused on the knowing gaze of the older woman, and he was suddenly aware of a precious presence he could not name. But, indeed, it lasted only a moment, and then it was gone, as he continued following her words. "I heard my own grandfather knew a lot 'bout such things; never knew him. Shame the way people don't get along, with so much to offer each other."

Her recent excitement over concern for Abel's coat had cost Grace, weak as she was, too much energy. Abel, noticing her sudden shortness of breath, cautioned her, "Now you take it easy, Grace. Not so much talking. In fact, it'd be best if you just try to get some more rest."

Abel got up to soak the cloth strips in the hot, medicinal water; and, after hanging four of them over a fairly long, strong stick he had picked up by the campfire, he brought them to Grace, who, as before, kept a diligent eye on his activity. "Grace, I need to place these on your forehead, neck and chest. Please bear with me."

"You go 'head—and do what—needs to be done," returned Grace. "Only, talk to me, Abe. Where are you from?"

"I'll talk if you promise just to listen. Your fever's higher now. You need to rest and stay quiet to restore your energy." When Grace nodded her willingness to comply, Abel stooped down and placed the first cooled strip of cloth across his patient's forehead.

At that moment, William arrived back on the scene, dustier than he had left, unsuccessful in his "critter" hunt, with shoulders hunched and empty-handed.

CHAPTER ELEVEN

"I'm mostly from around here." Abel began sharing his requested history. Grace lay resting next to the small log he was seated on at the campsite. "My mother was Indian, as you say, Grace. She was of the Nimiipuu people, the Nez Perce, who live northwest of here, on a plain unmatched for its beauty. Her name was Dancing Star."

"Dancing Star!" William, seated on the ground next to his mother, straightened his thin torso with an upward wiggle. "I like that name, Abe! Sure is pretty."

"Mm-hmm." Abel smiled at William. "I think so, too." Abel could see that Grace wanted to make her own comment, but he put an index finger to his smiling lips to silently remind her, "No talking allowed," before he continued. "And she was the daughter of a chief."

"You makin' this up?" William's eyes narrowed.

"No, William, I promise it's true. Every clan has its leader, and he's the chief. And, as it turned out, my mother was the daughter of one of them."

"Bet she was pretty as her name, huh, Abe?" It seemed William's doubt had flown.

Grace, whose eyes were now closed, smiled at the comment and nodded her agreement.

"My father and grandfather, and some who knew her," Abel went on, "told me she was very beautiful, but when I try to recall her at my bedside or preparing a meal, I can see only her form. Her features are shadowy now."

Abel noticed then that Grace's chills were getting worse, and he turned to his young friend. "William, hand me the thick blanket you brought from my bedroll, will you?"

"Sure." William jumped up.

As soon as William handed him the blanket, Abel took it and formed it into a neat, pillowy cushion. Then addressing Grace, he said, "The medicine will do its work, but I can't put too many blankets on you while you've got this fever. I know you're uncomfortable, Grace, but maybe this will help." He gently lifted her head and placed the fluffed bundle beneath it.

Grace gazed at him with gratitude, then closed her eyes again as Abel and William took their positions, sitting near, on either side of her.

Abel relaxed, peace filling him at the sight of his two new friends. Indeed, he felt glad that circumstances had brought him among them to give what he could, but also, he was affected by the uncommon generous spirit he observed in their natures.

Presently, William broke the silence. "Somethin' wrong, Abe?"

Abel glanced up from the twigs he had been fiddling with in his hands. "Huh? No. I don't want to disturb your ma, is all. She finally seems settled in and doesn't need me keeping her from sleep that'll do her good."

"Please go on, Abe," Grace half-whispered. "You'll know I'm tired of listenin' when you hear me snorin' away." But just then, her eyes narrowed as she gazed weakly toward Abel, her tone sharp. "You best keep a lookout for my older boy. That one could be trouble; hate to say it 'bout my own."

Abel wondered at her sudden concern as he glanced inquisitively from Grace to William.

But Grace had already taken on a lighter tone. "Now, Mr. Abe from mostly 'round here, I wanna hear all 'bout you. If you want me to rest at ease, please go on."

Abel, bemused, raised an eyebrow and, with a slight smile of consent, resumed his story. He swept through some lighthearted childhood memories about his parents that he kept close to his heart. He started to falter as he pressed through the telling of his mother's tragic death, only half-noticing his listeners still attending him.

Presently, he felt a warm comfort rest on him, and opening his eyes, he met those of Grace, deep and black.

"I am sorry, Abe. Didn't mean to stir up such hurtful memories," said Grace. William, too, wore an apologetic look.

Abel waved his hand. "Please don't feel badly. I live with it, same as I'm sure your hearts hold their own heavy scars. It's been my experience that most people have dark memories to contend with," Abel said. "Neither of you had any fault in what befell my family," he added, nodding toward William, who perked up a bit. "You do me, instead, a real kindness. I guess my parents have just been on my mind a lot lately. And here the both of you are, with two pairs of listening ears."

Grace shivered again. Abel brought more water to her and replaced her medicinal cotton strips with freshly soaked ones, then pulled her quilt and blanket up to her shoulders. "I don't suppose you've got much of an appetite." Grace shook her head weakly. He coaxed her to drink a little more water, after which sleep overtook her.

Then, he motioned to William. "Come on. Let me show you how to cook a special broth that'll be good for your ma. Ol' white man's recipe." Abel winked. "It's called chicken soup." They laughed together.

"Hey," said William, following Abel to his horse, "where you gonna find a chicken out here?"

"Got some in my saddle pouch," Abel glanced back at William, who had just about gained on him. "I have a friend who does magic with chicken. Wife of Lieutenant Morris back at Fort Laramie." He stopped in his tracks and turned to William with an unmistakable gleam in his eyes. "Assisted by her pretty seventeen-year-old daughter, Ginny." Abel's heart lurched.

"You sure looked happy, Abe, when you talked 'bout Ginny just then." William grinned.

What William could not see was that behind Abel's gleam was his hard realization that a relationship with Ginny, free from the often dangerous difficulties of discrimination because of his Indian status–even if his fondness for her *was* reciprocated–was, for both of them, as far from possible as touching the stars could have been.

Without pause, Abel turned toward Artemis, right in front of them now, and laid his hand on a bulging saddle pouch. "They packed me a whole chicken before I left—big one, too—with plenty of salt to keep it from spoiling and two large loaves of fresh-baked bread. And that's not all. Mmm-mm!"

Abel winked at William, whose eyes were wide and lips were smacking at the mention of the tasty provisions. "Let's just say that Mrs. Morris assures the troops are well stocked when they're sent out." The portion of Abel's fare that he produced for William's inspection consisted of a jar of preserved, sliced, yellow cling peaches, a jar of blueberry jam, ten flat sticks of dried, salted beef jerky, a block of hard, white cheese, and three, polished red apples.

"Yeah, but you're just one man, Abe!" blurted out William, his eyes at their widest, as Abel replaced the food in his saddlebag.

"Exactly," Abel said. "Lucky me, and lucky you." Then Abel drew out from the other compartment of his saddlebag a plump package wrapped in brown paper and tied with a string. "Soon as I prepare the broth for your ma, we'll have some food ourselves."

When the broth was ready, Abel brought it to Grace; but as she slipped in and out of consciousness, she could not take in very much. Abel saw the boy's worried face as William leaned over his mother. "She's pretty bad right now, William. But she's going to make it. The medicine's good. And we caught the fever right at the onset." These words seemed to ease William's anxiety.

"Thank you, Abe," he whispered.

The day fell into evening as Abel and William tended to Grace. They fed her more of the broth and water at intervals, while Abel took true delight in watching William feast. Abel decided that after Grace's fever broke, they would let her rest for another day before traveling to Fort Laramie, where she could get the medical attention that would help her to recuperate fully. Besides, Abel reasoned, they could stretch the food a few days, and he could hunt small game nearby to add to their larder. He hoped that Jake had not met with some mishap along the way and would be back before the next midday. At any rate, they could not delay any longer than a day or two more before starting the journey.

In the time that ensued until dark, William and Abel got to know each other better. Abel was moved by an awareness that he was gaining esteem in the boy's young heart, and this through what he considered the simplest, most natural endeavors on his part. But if this was so, that growing esteem was mutual. He gave William the duty of feeding oats to Artemis twice during the remainder of that long day. William assisted him, too, by pouring the canteen water carefully into Abel's cupped hands whenever he gave Artemis a drink at the campground. Adding to William's obvious earnest eagerness to be of help, for the most part, when Abel was at a task, each conversation and lighthearted rambling between the two served to deepen Abel's peace.

As soon as the sun had set, however, Abel ordered William to bed after discovering he had not been to sleep in more than twenty-four hours. The boy slept soundly while Abel sat by Grace, kept the fire going, and applied newly soaked strips of cloth when she needed them.

But finally, good news. As the sun peaked over the eastern horizon, Grace's fever broke as he had expected. Eager to tell William, he raced over to the boy and, crouching beside the outstretched form, he tapped William's shoulder. "Hey, buddy," he whispered just loud enough to startle. "The fever's broke. Your ma's going to be fine. She just needs lots of rest."

William rubbed his eyes and blinked hard. "Yeah?"

"You bet. Go see for yourself."

The lad scurried from his bedroll to his mother's side and touched her cool, moist face.

"She'll be sleeping soundly for a while," Abel said. "Her body's had to fight through a lot."

"You're some doctor, Abe!"

"You're not so bad yourself, guy. Your ma's awfully lucky to have a son with a bedside manner like yours." Abel gave William a pat on the back. Then speaking to himself, he added, "Guess I should refill the canteens. She'll be thirsty when she wakes up."

"Right away," said William as he went for the canteens.

"No hurry. The sun'll be brighter soon. You'll see better then."

"Pa always said I got eyes like a owl," William proclaimed, scooping up the canteens. "I'll be right back."

"Whoa, William. Why don't you untether Artemis and ride her there? Get you there a little faster, and you won't have to tote back the full canteens on foot."

"You're kiddin'! You'll let me take her by myself?"

"Why not? You do know how to ride a horse, don't you?"

"Yeah, but this one sure seems special." William's eyes widened.

"She's special, all right, and I can tell she's taken a liking to you." Abel nodded at his friend. "Doesn't happen with just anyone. Besides, she'll appreciate a nice, long morning drink at the creek while you fill the canteens. Take the oats with you, too. You already know the amount to feed her. How 'bout it, buddy?"

"You bet! You can count on me, Abe! We won't take too long," William said, and he headed for Artemis, his chest out, his smile wide. As soon as Abel and William re-saddled Artemis, the boy mounted and urged the horse into a fast walk.

Gratified, Abel watched William disappear, proudly astride Artemis.

In less than half an hour, William returned to the campsite with filled canteens, a contented horse, and the smile of a newly minted horseman.

CHAPTER TWELVE

From earlier discussions between Abel and his young companion, Abel learned more about the Pearce family, especially William. Where William had been suspect before, Abel ascertained that however charming and easygoing the boy may have been, he also had an unfortunate penchant on the plantation where the Pearces had lived and had been formerly owned, for getting himself into trouble. Abel suspected that William was apt to follow his own inclinations whenever certain impish high winds teased coaxingly over his inquisitive character.

Among the tales told, one involved Miss Marilyn, the fifteen-year-old niece of the landowner, Mr. Pierce Butler. One afternoon, she was carrying, in the large, uplifted fold of her apron, a bunch of hand-picked flowers to her beau who had come to call. The young suitor had been seated on the wide, marble porch steps of the manor, where he had been instructed to wait, as the girl approached him from a distance.

William, then eight years old, seeing the leafy array of petals bouncing gaily over the fringe of the girl's apron, had bolted forward to see the treasure she was delivering.

"Miss Marilyn! Miss Marilyn! Whatcha got there?" William had called.

The unsuspecting flower-bearer all at once had turned toward the approaching boy who had left his work to chase his own inescapable interest.

"William, stop!" Miss Marilyn had shouted, halting where she was.

Startled, William had tripped on a long stone in his path and fell, toppling directly upon her.

The young man on the porch had hurried to the aid of his disheveled damsel and demanded, "That clumsy boy should be punished!"

Marilyn, having grown up with William since she was very young, was among the many who had a natural soft spot for him and had been less inclined to recommend the harsher punishments for William's infringements. Still, she could not let such a chivalrous moment escape, even at the boy's expense.

Her beau had insisted that William receive three lashes in her presence to repair the disgrace he caused the young lady and that he apply better to his duties from then on. At the direction of Marilyn's suitor, the boy was straightaway lashed three substantial strokes by the overseer and sent back to his work.

When William was nine, he had received five lashes simultaneously across both of his slender arms after examining a new, beautifully painted, porcelain vase as it was unloaded from a buckboard. Before William finished his inspection, the vase lay on the ground in pieces. A far worse chastisement, Abel was told, had been dealt to the slave who unwittingly allowed William to hold the vase.

Another time, William had climbed a tree to rescue a stray cat trapped on one of the higher limbs. He was cautioned by an overseer to come down before he was hurt and to leave the cat to its fate. Well, William did come down— straight down—the short way, after losing his grip on a branch, but not before he had the cat securely in hand. The cat landed safely, protected within the sheltering fold of William's arms.

Unfortunately, William's right leg had been broken in the fall. This meant he was on the mend for several months, thus would not be of much use in the fields during that time. Seven lashes were administered to add to the pain of his injury, as well as for foolishly disobeying the overseer's order. That had been over a year ago, just before his eleventh birthday. He shared with Abel that he was just happy not to be looking over his shoulder at a whip every time one of his "slight mistakes" resulted in a mini-disaster.

From William, Abel also learned of the family's heartache when Grace's husband, Thaddeus, was abducted by slave-catchers in Chicago and illegally returned, so the family concluded, to the South by force. Once there, he undoubtedly would have been sold again into slavery, as had happened even to many freeborn blacks.

Abel's heart clenched as he listened to the plight of William's family, but beyond this, there was, perhaps oddly, a certain empathy with, and solicitude for, the absent Jake that grew quite naturally the more he learned of him. At one point, after evening and silence had fallen on the little camping group, while Grace slumbered with only intermittent awakenings to drink a little broth or water, the topic of Jake was reopened in the following way.

Abel's young friend shuffled some pebbles in the dirt with his shoes. He put his hands in his pockets and shrugged his shoulders, eyeing the dusty bits of stone he had pushed deeper into the ground.

Abel watched him, curiosity furrowing his brow. "Got something you want to say, William?"

"It's about Jake," William started.

"You're worried about him, huh, buddy?"

"Yeah, well," he hesitated, "it ain't exactly that."

"What then, William?" Abel waited a moment for William to unburden his apparent worry. "Maybe we can sort things out if you tell me what it's about."

"Well, Abe," William pushed out the words, still eyeing the stony ground, "see Jake, he's got a passionate hate for white folks." William looked up from the ground toward Abel. "I mean, it's somethin' fierce, Abe. You'd see it plain if you knew him." The boy's eyes dropped again. "Ma says Pa could always tell the good men from the bad but not Jake. He calls 'em hypocrites who try to show him a good turn and hates them worst of all." William locked eyes on Abel. "Mama says hate's like a disease that

66

suffocates a man and makes his life useless, with no room for anythin' else."

"Your ma's right, William," Abel readily affirmed. "But I can understand your brother, too."

William scrunched his nose and eyebrows inquisitively. "You can?"

"I'm part Indian, remember?" Abel paused. "And I've had some trouble myself."

William paused, looking away a moment or two, and then went on, "Indians ain't much liked where we come from neither." Then he added as if surrendering hope, "So I guess you hate 'em, too. Whites, I mean."

Abel shook his head. "You forget; I'm only half-Indian. William, you seem to know some white folks are good, but lots also look down on others for one reason or another. Same's true of all folks, no matter what their color. I've had experiences with both. Fact is, many of those who only show their bad side have plenty of good in them that they just don't know how to let out, and some aren't given a real chance. My pa taught me that truth."

"Do you really believe that, Abe?" William crouched down beside Abel.

"I do now. But I can't lie; I have to tell you, there've been times I just couldn't see it. And even though deep down I know better, still sometimes it takes a lot of effort to hang on to that belief."

William drew a deep breath and slowly released it. "Ma and me pray for Jake a lot.

67

Alita Ngo

Mama says there ain't nothin' else left to do that'll bring him any good."

"I see." Abel was quiet for a moment. "You weren't by any chance worried about my being here when your brother returns?"

"I didn't know you was half-Indian, Abe!" William burst forth. "And even if Jake does see it, it won't make no difference. He's a lot bigger than you, Abe, and...you said yourself Ma's gonna get better. And Jake'll be here tomorrow for sure, I know it. We'll be fine; really, we will, Abe. We made it this far, ain't we? Couldn't you just—"

"No, William. I'm afraid it's not that simple," Abel interrupted. "Now that I've found you, I can't just leave you and go on my merry way, trusting that Jake'll return before the two of you starve, or something else terrible befalls you out here. I can't do that," he said pointedly. "I appreciate the warning, but I promise I'll be watchful."

William must have seen that Abel was in earnest and immovable; he lowered his eyes and nodded. "Guess I'll be leavin' it in God's hands like Ma taught me." He looked up at Abel again. "Ma's been sayin' that a lot lately."

68

CHAPTER THIRTEEN

William rose. "I'll go check on Artemis before I turn in, so you won't have to, Abe. Maybe she'll like a little moonlight grazin', if that'd be all right."

"That'd be great. Thanks for offering." Abel smiled, though a knot tightened in his gut. As William walked away, Abel stood and stretched a minute, shaking out his limbs and twisting his torso at the waist, until a small surge of new energy revitalized him. Then he reached into his right pocket and pulled out a doubled string of polished, milky-amber agate beads. The attached, filed brass crucifix revealed it was a rosary. He sauntered over to his bedroll, which was already laid out for the night, and re-seated himself in a comfortable position. Starting with the Sign of the Cross, he began reciting the rosary prayers, imperceptibly to any onlooker but for the movement of his lips silently forming words as he slipped one smooth, round bead after the next between his right forefinger and thumb, with the crucifix held in his right palm. When he was near the end of his recitation, he detected William's slight footfalls approach from behind.

"Say, Ma's got one of them," William piped up as he leaned over Abel's left shoulder, pointing to the rosary.

"She has a rosary?" Abel twisted around to catch William's gaze. "Your family's Catholic?

Funny, your ma didn't say anything when I mentioned that I was."

Evidently unmindful that he had interrupted Abel's prayer, William found a spot next to him and his words continued to fly. But, in fact, Abel was caught in a genuine curiosity to hear the new detail.

"Ma likes visitin' different churches when we're able to. The Cath'lic ones got a pull on her when she enters 'em, she says. I know what she means. She says they got a solemn presence the others ain't got...somethin' that's bigger than all the people inside. 'Most all of 'em's white, 'course, and we ain't allowed into the services, 'cept in a separate place like in the basement, but Ma says that'll change. People just gotta start seein' things like God sees 'em and with more courage. If folks had more courage 'bout what they knew was right in the first place, Ma says, things'd change a whole lot faster."

Abel nodded, having no better light to shed upon the subject.

William paused and bent his head toward the object Abel was still holding. "What did you call it again?"

"A rosary."

"Yeah, a ros'ry. So you know all the prayers, then. Ma and me only know *The Lord's Prayer.* Jake knows that one, too. How many you need to know to do all the beads, Abe?" William leaned closer.

"Well, besides the beginning and ending prayers, you only need to know the *Our Father*

70

and two shorter ones, and you repeat them as you go around the circle." Abel demonstrated, holding up the rosary and passing a section of the beads quickly through the loose grasp of his fingers and thumbs. "Where'd your ma get her rosary, if I might ask?" Abel cocked an eyebrow.

"When we was in Chicago, Ma took me with her to visit a Cath'lic church that was just built. I remember it was called Holy Family Church 'cause it was almost Christmas when we went to see it. 'Majestic' is what Ma called it. It was so high! Just reachin' up to God!" William illustrated by extending both arms as far upwards as he could manage in his sitting position, letting the tips of his two index fingers meet in a point, and staring up at the imaginary steeple before bringing his hands back down to rest in his lap. Then turning toward Abel once more, William detoured from his discourse. "S'pose you been in a lot of 'em, huh, Abe, you bein' Cath'lic and all?"

Abel replied, "I was in a small, loghouse church at a mission when I was no more than a baby, too young to remember. Aren't any Catholic churches in this territory yet, buddy, but I know of some good priests who are bound to build them."

"Not in Sacramento, either?" William's voice dropped low.

"Sacramento? Is that where you're headed?" Abel turned up a smile. "Sacramento's a different story. If there's not a Catholic church in that city, I'll be surprised. Not as 'majestic'

71

as your Chicago church, I'm afraid, but beautiful, too, I'm sure." Abel paused as he formed an idea. "We'll have to talk more about this later," he said with a whimsical grin. Then he poured his rosary beads into the palm of his right hand and returned the rosary to his pocket.

William straightened. "Oh, yeah, the rosary! I almost forgot...when we was leavin' the church that day, a lady dressed real pretty, standin' close to Ma, bent down and picked up a ros'ry from the ground. She must've thought Ma dropped it 'cause she smiled and put it in Ma's hand and rushed off with her child before Ma could return it or say anythin'. That's how she got the ros'ry, Abe. The place was real crowded and no tellin' who the ros'ry really belonged to." William took a breath and shrugged his shoulders.

"In those circumstances, I'd say it was fair enough for her to hang onto it," Abel commented.

"That's what I told her. It seemed like it'd been used a lot, but still good and strong; just a plain wood ros'ry with a wood cross and a little Jesus attached to it."

Abel smiled at the boy's delightful and refreshing simplicity.

"Ma has a special pocket sewed into her skirt where she keeps it," William continued, "so that she don't go nowhere without it, and no one can think to take it from her."

"Good thinking on her part, William," Abel responded.

"Tell you what, then, when we get to Fort Laramie, I'll write out those other prayers for your ma on a piece of paper; then she can teach them to the rest of the family, and that way all of you can say the Rosary together whenever you like." Abel lingered over a thought. "We used to do that when my ma was alive. Pa had told me it took him some getting used to." Abel chuckled softly to himself. "Then later, Pa and I kept it up. Now I say it alone from time to time. I don't know; it helps. Still, praying together's an encouraging thing, especially with family. Brings you closer to each other and to knowing God and His goodness.

"We'd sure like havin' those prayers, Abe. Ma 'specially."

"Happy to oblige her, buddy. Now, I guess it's time we join your ma and get some shut-eye ourselves." Then Abel rose, yawned and stretched out his arms, and bent down to dust off the legs of his trousers.

"I'm all for that." Following his friend's lead, William situated himself in his own bedding, a few feet from Abel's. Lying not far from the fire, Abel watched with tired eyes the flickering flames as they sent golden lights dancing among the shadows playing over Grace's sleeping form on the other side of the campfire pit. Above him, a moonless sky showed off its spectacular dome of stars as a soft, cool wind blew through the camp. The chirping of crickets, the call of the Great Gray Owl perched somewhere nearby, and the howls of distant coyotes mingled together in what could have

73

been, as far as Abel was concerned, a lullaby sweetly sung to bring on welcome slumber. In another instant, he would have been asleep.

"Hey, Abe," came a low, hesitant whisper.

"Hmm? What is it, buddy?" asked Abel, drowsily.

"Where'd you get *your* ros'ry?"

"It was my ma's," Abel replied. Then, slowly, he turned on his other side so that he faced William and propped himself slightly on his elbow. "Father De Smet, he's the priest who married my ma and pa, and he's the one who gave the rosary to my ma after the wedding. He gave her a small, beautiful card, too, with a picture of the Holy Family. But the card was destroyed later in a fire. That's when the rosary came to me. That's the story, William." Abel smiled softly and rolled back into his former position, fixing his blanket over his shoulder. "Now we'd better both get some sleep, or your ma'll be the one tending to us in the morning, instead of the other way around. 'Night, William," said Abel, yawning again.

"Goodnight, Abe," returned William, his voice lighthearted and contented.

CHAPTER FOURTEEN

On the morning of July 14th, the beginning of Abel's third day at the Pearce camp, while William and Grace were still sound asleep, Abel had risen early to ride Artemis out to the familiar creek, where he fed her some oats and let her drink from the cool, clear water. A refreshing breeze rustled the low-hanging leaves of a nearby tree, and the chattering of a few birds mingled with Artemis' quiet neighs as she drank the delicious water in that serene spot. Abel desired to stay longer but thought it better to return to the camp as soon as Artemis was tended to. He spoke softly, as was his way, and patted her neck affectionately before mounting her and riding the short trek back to camp.

Finding William just awake, Abel fixed and then shared a friendly breakfast of fried bacon and warmed biscuits spread with Mrs. Morris' mouth-watering blueberry preserves, after which both felt caught in a welcome tiredness. Neither spoke, as a few luscious moments of silence ensued, crowned with the victors' cognizance that Grace had slept peacefully all night.

Upon refueling the campfire, the boys moved far enough from Grace so that her sleep would not be disturbed by their voices. William sat leaning against the trunk of a cottonwood, spinning a sharp stone between his two index fingers with his thumbs. Abel stood, a few yards opposite him, with his back resting on the wall of rock he sat against during his watch the night before. He lifted a leg and wedged the sole of his boot in a low, shallow niche of the rock, his hands in his pockets. As he took in the details of the morning's sights and sounds, he caught sight of William's scrunched up sleeve, bearing his whip scars. Abel instinctively winced.

"They bother you a lot, huh, Abe?" The boy apparently noticed what had caused his friend's reaction.

"Those stripes?" Abel nodded toward the marks on William's arms. "Yes, they do." He removed his hands from his pockets and folded his arms in front of him. "I can't help it, William. It's not right; it shouldn't—"

"It shouldn't've happened to a little kid?" William finished Abel's sentence. "It shouldn't happen if you're old or at your strongest neither, ain't that right?" William shifted his position.

"No argument," Abel said.

The lad discarded the pointy rock, picked up a smaller, more rounded stone, and tumbled it back and forth in both hands. "What I was going to say, William, is it shouldn't be tolerated that the powerful— " Abel hung his head and shook it slowly. "You sure don't need me explaining to you."

Abel took off his hat and pushed back his dark hair which had fallen partly in front of his eyes. Then looking up into the blueness of the sky, he mused aloud. "Real power's not what they make it out to be. Can't be."

Young William hardly had been listening. "Funny thing" —he almost chuckled— "I 'spect I got 'most as many of these whip marks as Jake's got, but it seems like his whippings hurt him a lot more than mine did." William paused and tossed the stone overhand about ten feet away. "Guess he got hit a whole lot harder." The boy swept a side glance at Abel. "You s'pose?" His words seemed to beg for an honest answer.

"You're smart for a young fella, William," Abel returned with a kind smile, replacing his hat on his head. "Wish I had been that smart when I was your age."

"Heck, I ain't smart. My pa's smart. He knows 'bout a lot of stuff. And he can figure his way 'round or out of most things. He don't give up, neither. 'Givin' up ain't smart'; Pa says that a lot." The boy fell silent a moment, then resumed more brightly. "And my ma, she's wise. I reckon my ma's 'bout the wisest person I'll ever meet. She just knows things, Abe. That's how I trust we'll be gettin' Pa back; Ma says she knows it."

William seemed so set in the conviction of his mother's wisdom that Abel could not doubt it. Already, he had noted Grace's gift of insight. Moreover, he did not miss that William had inherited her gift. William spoke nobly, too, of his father, and Abel wished he had known him.

"You're lucky to have the ma you do. Your pa would be proud of how you and your brother

77

are looking out for her." Abel reached down to pick up a short, dry piece of cottonwood limb. He pulled a sharp, hand-sized knife from its scabbard near his bootstrap and began to whittle the stump of wood.

"Yeah, huh?" William smiled. "We're gonna get him back, Abe. I know we'll be together again. Then maybe Jake'll stop bein' so angry."

Abel surmised from what he now knew of Jake, that everything in him raged against belonging to a master, although he was forced to comply in consideration of his parents and their safety. Jake, William had reported, had seen them both under the whip because of his defiance toward the landowner. That was when he was much younger but old enough to work on Butler's Island, the name of the Georgia cotton plantation owned by the wealthy Pierce Butler. Moreover, a particular overseer seemed to have it in for the burly youth. William was different, with a natural charm and easiness that had won the attention and even, one might venture to say, the mild affection of the whites of the manor. It seemed his whippings were invariably the result of mishaps due to a remarkably curious nature and an impetuous passion for engaging in the life that swelled around him even amidst the baneful hand that had been dealt him and his family.

Abel continued to carve the broken limb of wood. "Do you have a plan for recovering your pa?"

"Don't know yet." William shook his head. "We ain't had time to figure it out. But we'll get him back all right. Ma says right now, what we gotta do is just keep headin' west to a place called Sacramento and keep our thoughts on Pa. The good Lord'll do what we can't."

Abel stopped a moment, held the carving up to the sunlight, examining the evolving sculpture, and posed another question. "Did you and your family always live on the same plantation, the one you were born on?"

The boy sat up alert and leaned in confidentially. "Me and Jake, and even Ma and Pa, was born on Butler's Island. But we lived on the Melrose Plantation in Mississippi when we came to be freed. That's the plantation we worked on after Mr. Butler sold us, same time he sold most of his other slaves, the winter before last. I remember it was rainin' mighty hard that day. The air was all thick and musty inside the back room of the big hall, 'cause of the amount of bodies pushed together, where we'd been waitin' since real early for the auction to start. We was the first slaves sold that day, though."

"Seems drastic on Butler's part, his selling all his slaves at once." Abel tapped the butt of his knife against his thigh, releasing the bits of wood shavings that clung to the blade.

"Pa said Mr. Butler was broke from gamblin' so much, and he was forced to sell us, else he would've lost his land, sure. Lucky we wasn't separated like other families. Even Ma can't figure why Mr. Butler kept us together," William puzzled. "We was first up on the block the day we was sold, like I said, and Mr.

79

McMurran, the owner of the Melrose Plantation, didn't waste no time buyin'. Out-bid the only other man who seemed bent on takin' us with him. Sure glad that one didn't take us home; I didn't like the looks of him—worse even than Mr. Butler. The McMurrans turned out nicer than Mr. Butler. Anyways, I don't reckon we would've got free if the man biddin' against Mr. McMurran would've won. Like I said, he was powerful, scary lookin', and he kept a-swearin' like I ain't never heard."

"My pa talked about slavery," replied Abel. "He called it a malicious, Godless way for human beings to treat other human beings." Abel had felt a troubling mixture of ire and helplessness as William spoke of the auction.

"We ain't white. That's all there's to it."

"No, William. A thing like that's got to change, and it may be sooner than you think. I hope you live to see it ended."

"You and me both," William added.

Abel broke a smile. "You and me both."

A solemn quiet was unbroken for several minutes until William spoke. "I know you're half-white yourself, Abe, but I gotta ask."

Abel held the knife still in one hand and the animal carving that was taking shape in the other. "What's on your mind, buddy?"

"Well, yesterday when I was tellin' you 'bout the way Jake felt, you said you'd had some trouble like Jake's. So I was wonderin'...well, I was wonderin', do white folks treat you bad 'cause you're part Indian?"

"That always depends." Abel cut a deep groove along the top of the cottonwood creature he was bringing to life and slid his knife smoothly across the length of the limb he held, peeling away a portion of the wood, which fell among the small pile of shavings accumulating on the ground next to him.

"Depends on what?"

"On the white person and how he sees things."

Both William's eyebrows lifted. "Where we come from, they all seem to see things pretty much the same. I mean, some's meaner than others, but there don't seem to be a lot of difference in the way they think 'bout slaves. Anyways, none I met 'cept Miss Fannie."

Suddenly, it was Abel whose curiosity heightened. "Oh? Who's she?"

"She used to be Mr. Butler's wife, till she couldn't stand him no more. He brought her back from England on one of his trips there. Ma says she was a stage actress—somebody important's all I know. Guess she didn't have experience with plantation slaves till she got to Butler's Island."

"That why they didn't get along, Butler and his new wife?" Abel asked. "Because she didn't like what she saw with the slaves?"

William nodded. "She was always puttin' in a word to the master for those who was mistreated or sick. He didn't like that." The boy's eyes gleamed as he disclosed a bit of intrigue. "And she taught my ma to read and write." Abel listened intently to William's story.

81

"No lying, Abe; Miss Fannie taught a small bunch of the women house slaves to read and write. Ma says the Lord blessed her by makin' her one of the chosen ones that Miss Fannie helped to better 'emselves."

Abel momentarily stopped whittling and rested his forearms against his knees, while William continued.

"But the mistress had to do it in secret so's to protect those women, 'cause if her husband would've found out, he would've been mighty angry and took it out on 'em. But Miss Fannie was smart, and he never found out."

Abel peered at William with piqued interest. "What happened then? You said she *used to be* his wife."

"Things got real bad between 'em. Ma said Miss Fannie finally took off and sent him papers to get a divorce. Ma was sad when she left, but she said she could see it comin' and asked the Lord's blessin' on the pretty white lady who was so good to all our families," William concluded. "Is that the kind of white people you're talkin' 'bout, Abe?"

"Yes, William. I guess you'd say Miss Fannie's one of the white people who looks at things differently than most. Sounds like a good lady who married the wrong guy."

"You're tellin' me!" William's eyebrows stretched almost to the top of his hairline as he shook his head coolly.

Abel peered sideways at the boy and grinned, then resumed his whittling. "You suppose the mistress had any say in your family staying together?" inquired Abel.

"They were already divorced," William said.

Abel shrugged. "Maybe keeping her favorite family intact eased Butler's regret."

"Can't hardly 'magine him bein' regretful 'bout anythin'"

"You never know all the secrets of a man's heart, buddy. Just isn't possible."

"Maybe it's so; I don't know. Still, it don't seem likely, regret and Mr. Butler ever goin' hand in hand."

Continuing to curl shavings from his stump of wood, Abel brought the conversation back to William's mother. "So your ma can read and write. Guess it never occurred to me she might not be able to read those Rosary prayers I promised to write down. I don't wonder at my presumption, though; not with her."

"Sure, she can read. And she's been tryin' to teach me little by little as she's been able," William said, jumping into the next thought. "Practically know all the twenty-six letters of the alphabet and can write 'em, too." The lad puffed out his chest like plumage in a show of heartfelt pride over his newly earned and notably important skill. "We practice in the dirt with a stick sometimes, so I won't forget."

"Sure. She wants you to have the best possible opportunities like every good ma does." Abel left off whittling and looked seriously at his young friend. "And remember, buddy, your being able to read and write is a valuable thing to those around you, too." The blade of his knife caught glints from the sun as Abel pointed its tip toward the distance. "Why I know plenty of white people, women, and men, too, who can't read a word. Never take it lightly. Your ma's giving you a powerful gift, just like Miss Fannie did for her."

William leaned forward with another question. "Where'd you learn your letters, Abe?"

"My pa taught me to read and write and calculate in English; he'd been a schoolteacher, you know."

"A schoolteacher?" William's head tilted.

"Yep," Abel replied, a hint of pride in his voice. "My grandpa taught me Nez Perce. Even picked up a little Shoshoni and Cayuse on my own; those are Indian peoples I've had a good share of contact with." Abel paused. "Once you start learning, it's kind of like trying to steer a runaway horse." Abel positioned his hands as if they were gripping the flying mane of an invisible stallion. "But you just keep holding onto the reins, William, and that horse'll take you places you never even dreamed of."

Abel held up the horse he had been sculpting. The horse had been carved in a swift and graceful running pose, and its mane and tail were waving in an imaginary wind.

William's eyes shot wide open. They were riveted on the handsomely finished wooden stallion. "Ah, Abe! Can I see?"

Abel plunked the carved horse down into William's carefully cupped hands.

84

William lifted and twisted the small stallion slowly, first one way, then the other, examining it eagerly. Then he ran a finger over the curves and creases of solid grain Abel had fashioned from the deadwood.

"It's beautiful, Abe!"

"It's yours," said Abel.

William beamed with pleasure, then continued to admire the masterpiece. "Will you teach me to carve like that?"

"'Course I'll teach you," replied Abel, returning his knife to its scabbard. "I admit I never had quite such a favorable reaction to one of my carvings. I do them for fun. Sure am glad you like it, buddy."

"Like it? I sure do. Thanks, Abe!"

"You know, William," Abel nodded toward the token. "I have to admit, I've never seen anything as beautiful and fascinating as a wild horse galloping freely across the plains." And musing, he brought to mind his sojourns on the plains of the northwestern Dakota Territory, just east of the Continental Divide, a couple of summers together with his grandfather and the Nez Perce, during their annual buffalo hunts. During these hunts, too, Abel had the privilege to witness the occasional wild herd of horses rushing, noble and magnificent, across the open land. For the moment, he was back there among them again.

CHAPTER FIFTEEN

As Abel rested in the late morning on his bedroll that same day, thoughts of his father's death came to the forefront of his mind. Together with his overwhelming grief following Elijah's violent death, the stark images and emotions surrounding the incident had sent Abel into a mental state where he had been difficult to reach. Laughing Thunder, who cared for Abel after the Shoshoni attack at the Wheaton farm, told him that joining the buffalo hunt would be good medicine. Abel spent most of his time brooding around the camp and was hard-pressed to follow the lead of other youths of the tribe who tried to involve him in their work, games, and hunting.

Although his mother's people, and especially his grandfather, were kind and attentive to Abel, showing no disparity between him and the rest of the clan, he could not resist feeling for some time that he was not only an orphan but an outsider. Abel's mother, Dancing Star, had been his grandfather's only child, whose own mother had died in childbirth. Laughing Thunder, Abel later realized, knew personally the deep pain of loss that had gripped his grandson.

So it followed that his grandfather had decided to involve Abel in the hunt the summer of 1855, only a few months after the tragedy. As

Laughing Thunder was the leader of the party, he was able to choose the braves who would hunt with him. Other young braves close in age to Abel also were chosen to join the hunting party.

In the excitement of the hunt, Abel's mind had been riveted on learning the buffalo hunting skills: how to ride swiftly alongside the great animals during the hunt; to aim an arrow precisely while at a gallop; and to harness a buffalo for transport back to the tribal camp.

Abel eagerly awaited the hunt the following summer; and after a second successful hunt, he had returned to the Indian camp with new pride in aiding the capture of buffalo that would feed and bring warmth and shelter to the people for another year. On their return from the second hunt, Laughing Thunder had presented his grandson with a beautiful Appaloosa, whom Abel named Artemis. His grandfather had traded three buffalo hides for the horse he had admired in the camp of a neighboring tribe. Abel was elated with the gift. From then on, he and Artemis were almost inseparable. He learned to ride her with speed and skill and to treat her with kindness and care; soon, their mutual bond set deeply.

Abel kept dear the memory of his loving grandfather close to his heart. Now Laughing Thunder was gone, too. The youth had left the Indian camp in the spring of 1857, striking out on his own, though only sixteen, with his grandfather's blessing. That following October his grandfather was killed during a battle with the Blackfoot, rivals of the Nez Perce on their buffalo hunts, but whose warriors' unexplained invasion into Laughing Thunder's camp had remained a mystery to Abel.

When news of his grandfather's death reached Abel several weeks after the attack on the tribe, Abel had been working six months as an assistant guide for the steady stream of settlers traveling to the Willamette Valley in the western part of the region that was to become the State of Oregon, or to the ranch land on the east side of the impressive volcanic mountains of the Cascade Range, which separates the pastoral farming lands and fir forests to the west from the high desert plains on the east.

As time passed, Abel had adapted well and responsibly to the life of an assistant trail guide. Having been hired at the Fort Laramie juncture of the Oregon Trail, he brought welcome and reliable assistance to guides who were with the traveling settlers since they departed from the start of the route at St. Joseph, Missouri. On one of his later trips, when it became apparent that an extra hand was sorely needed for the large group of settlers heading on to Sacramento at the Fort Hall juncture in southeastern Idaho, Abel stepped up to fill the need. The emigrant party, with their new assistant guide, continued southwest on the California Trail, thus coming to know, first hand, the rugged and magnificent grandeur of the Sierra Nevada.

For Abel, this busy schedule and close to constant travels through rugged natural majesty subdued the remembrance of deep hurts almost completely. Fortunately, too, although he felt the impermanence of every substantial support given him by birthright from his Maker, none of life's many lessons taught him by his mother, father, and grandfather, whether consoling or difficult to endure, were lost on Abel. He was well on his way to manhood by now; and though he was more alone than ever before, Abel had accumulated a lasting store of sheltering love in his breast, effecting in him a keen observance of the good in his life, in the people he met, and in nature's wondrous beauty surrounding him during and apart from his routines.

Growing inexplicably more restless, however, with his guide job as the months wore on, and after he had assisted several Basque families with the sheep they herded along the trail, Abel seriously began to think about operating a sheep farm. This intent was, in part, a testament to his mother's love for him. He often thought of Dancing Star's fondness for the shepherd boy in the Bible whose humble offerings had so pleased the Creator and for whom she had named her own son. Perhaps, then, Abel mused, shepherding is where peace for him would be found.

Finally, on a morning in mid-May 1859, one month after his eighteenth birthday, Abel bought ten sheep from a Basque family who had stopped overnight at Fort Laramie on their way to Oregon. He brought his new herd to a small ranch he had bought a week before near the fort. From that time until early in 1860, Abel lived peacefully and uneventfully on his ranch. His knowledge about sheep and of sheep ranching and tending his growing flock increased daily. His main revenue came from selling wool and meat to the U. S. Army and civilians at Fort Laramie.

Then in March 1860, handbills were posted at the fort advertising for riders for a new and daring venture proposed by the Russell, Majors & Waddell, Central Overland, California, and Pike's Peak Express Company or shortened to its enduring title, the Pony Express. Abel fit the specifications for recruits, from the age requirement to the riding experience, right down to weight and stature. Abel's answer to the call of the Pony Express, however, derived mainly from the mounting necessity in him to follow adventure and be part of something vital and thriving again. Strengthened by the quietude of his life on his small ranch and the care of his sheep for ten months, Abel felt a new stability that prepared him to take on the risks described in the Pony Express recruit handbills. Two days after reading a notice at Fort Laramie, Abel sold his land and sheep to a retired soldier at the fort and signed up to join this bold, uncompromising experiment in speedy mail delivery.

***

"Hey, Abe." William's voice sounded far away as Abel jogged himself out of memories. The boy sat in the shade of the cottonwood tree and Abel could see that he had been inspecting once more the details of his carved stallion

90

which seemed to run free in the wind. Surely—
Abel thought —the vision of William's father
likewise running free somewhere must have
filled the boy's imagination as he examined his
sculpted treasure.

"Hmm, William?" Abel lifted himself partway
from his bedroll and stretched out his arms and
hands skyward before getting up to join
William by the cottonwood, and he stooped
down beside him.

"Well, Abe," William started slowly. "I know
an awful thing happened to your ma, but you
ain't said nothing 'bout your pa, where he is,
and what he's doin' now. Sure'd like to meet
him, if he's anything like you....I mean,
someday."

"You can't." Abel lowered his gaze. He felt
oddly shaken by the question. Then he glanced
up at his young friend who seemed hesitant to
talk any further. "My pa passed on about five
years ago."

"I'm sorry," said William, his voice dropping,
but his eyes fixed on Abel. "Was he sick?"

Abel's stomach clenched, but he took a deep
breath and exhaled. "William, I'm sorry; I just
can't talk about that right now. Things happen,
and...."

"That's okay, Abe," William stepped in. "Ain't
no need to apologize. I got a nose too long for
my face."

"What?" Abel grinned.

"That's what my pa always says; means I'm
too nosy." William projected an imaginary line
from the tip of his small nose to the end of his

91

right index finger extended at arm's length, then rolled his eyes for added effect.

Abel chuckled. "That's not necessarily a bad thing."

"Maybe." William shrugged. "But most times, it leads me to trouble."

Abel smiled and stood up. He patted his young companion lightly on the back, waving off any lingering aura of annoyance. "Guess we better look in on your ma and see how she's doing," Abel said, dusting off the thighs of his trousers.

William rose, too, the sparkle having returned to his eyes, and he walked with his friend, holding his handsome sculpture before him. "Yeah! And wait till she sees what you made me. That'll make her smile, sure 'nough." William scrutinized the carving anew as they approached Grace. "Think I'll name him Lightnin'. What do you think, Abe?"

"That's a fine name. It suits him." Abel playfully brushed his hand over William's neatly clipped, coarse, black hair, then swung his arm around the boy's shoulder and pulled him close, in the way a man hugs a little brother.

CHAPTER SIXTEEN

Grace's wide smile welcomed them as Abel and William strode to her side. "What've you two young men been up to? I could hear you carryin' on before I caught sight of you. How am I s'posed to rest if the doctors keep up such a racket?"

"Uh-oh. Looks like we're in for it now, William. I told you to quiet down back there." Abel winked at his partner in crime.

"You told me wha—? Oh, I get it. Sure," William obliged. "Sorry, Abe; sorry, Ma. You know I have trouble keepin' my mouth shut." After returning Abel's wink, he brought forth his treasure. "Hey, Ma, look what Abe made me! Whittled it out of wood. Ever know anybody who could whittle like that, Ma?" William handed her his prize. "Ain't he a beauty? I named him Lightnin'. Abe says it suits him."

Grace passed her hands over the curves and grooves of the artfully fashioned horse. "Can't think of a name that'd suit him better, son," replied Grace, admiring the carving before handing it back to William. "That's something you'll want to keep safe and take special pride in the rest of your life, young man," she added. Grace started to sit up, and Abel immediately supported her at her elbow and back.

"I never been so fussed over, 'cept the time my Thaddeus took care of me after...." She stopped herself and swept a hand before her eyes. "Ah, but that's history. Just look now, Abe, how the good Lord sends His angels where they're oftentimes least expected and most needed."

Grace glanced observantly at Abel. "Where'd you learn to carve such lovely things, son?"

"My mother's people. I spent some time with them after my father passed away," answered Abel.

"That right? Them bein' your mother's people, ain't they yours, too, Abe?"

"You're right, of course. It's just the way I talk, I guess: 'my mother's people,' 'my father's people.' Sounds a bit dramatic, I know, but at times I feel the two sides pulling at each other, kind of tearing me down the middle."

"Ever thought of havin' your two sides get acquainted and make friends with each other?" said Grace.

Abel raised an eyebrow. "No, ma'am. Haven't looked at it that way." He tilted his head slightly, making eye contact. "But it gives me something to think about." Then Abel asked, "But how are you feeling? That's what we came over to find out." He glanced at William for backup.

The boy crouched forward, elbows on his thighs and head propped on two supporting palms, listening attentively to the conversation. "That's right, Ma. But you sure look a whole lot better!"

"Don't I? You boys certainly are good doctors." Grace bunched up part of the thick blanket lying over her legs and lap and patted her hands on the mound she had formed in front of her. "Don't think I'll be dancin' any jigs just today, but here I am, sittin' up straight without gettin' dizzy. And that's a big improvement." Grace smiled, and Abel noted a new twinkle in her eyes.

"I'm glad to hear it. But be careful to take it slow; you're just mending, Grace, although before long, you'll be chasing this young man around again." Abel grinned and punched William gently on the arm.

***

Abel ensured that Grace had some nutrition after her serious depletion of sustenance during the last few days. Without pushing her to eat and drink more than was prudent all at once, he offered her a repeat of William's and his breakfast earlier that morning, but in a much smaller amount, and was delighted she was able to consume it all with no coaxing whatever. Then she settled for a nap.

As the day moved pleasantly on and the sun rose high in the midday sky, Abel again sat attentively at Grace's side. William had gone off in search of cottonwood pieces, big enough to start his carving lessons with Abel. Abel instructed him to bring back a fair amount from which to choose because they would need plenty of wood to practice with and sharpen William's skills.

95

When Grace woke up from her nap and had sat for a while resting, Abel leaned in. "I was wondering, Grace; I mean, if you don't mind my asking, how'd it happen with your husband?"

"You mean that boy of mine left somethin' unsaid?" Grace laughed. "Now you just settle down and let me tell you 'bout my Thad." As Grace opened her story, she had Abel's full attention.

"My Thad's a good man, big and powerful, too; Jake takes after him, though a mite taller than his pa, and both of 'em's dark as ebony; but mind you, my Thad knows what real gentleness and tenderness is." Grace wrapped her arms around herself, smiling. "Why, when he takes me in his strong arms, ain't no harm in this world can reach me; ain't no cruelty that can't be mended." She softly dropped her hands to her lap, and looking at Abel, her dark, sincere eyes spoke with her words. "Just can't tell you how much I miss him, Abe, and how fiercely I believe he'll get back to us safe." Grace paused and, with a gentle breath, began her tale. "But now let me tell you the story and how we tragic'ly lost him."

As Abel listened, the characters embedded in the detailed story told by Grace—what she lived, and all she later came to know of it— came alive in his imagination as if he had met each in the flesh. He duly gathered and stored the following facts surrounding the Pearce family's sad, and sometimes amazing, history. The story started in Savannah, Georgia, where Pierce Butler sold 429 of the slaves from his plantation to pay his gambling debts (as William had related), beginning on the rainy morning of March 2, 1859, and continuing into the next day. In order to bring in more buyers from a widespread area, Butler had posted the sale of his slaves in newspapers and handbills many weeks in advance, as far north as New York and as far west as Kansas. As a result of the advertising, buyers and buyers' representatives of various social levels attended the auction in Savannah. Although Butler was present, the auctioneers were in charge of moving the event smoothly and successfully along. By the end of the dehumanizing trade of human flesh, Butler had netted $300,000 and was financially solvent once more, for a while at least.

Appearing at the event at just the right moment, Mr. John T. McMurran, the well-known attorney and wealthy owner of the Melrose Manor in Natchez, Mississippi, had traveled to Butler's auction and was able to out-bid a brutish, foul-mouthed scalawag (the same mentioned earlier by William) who had an interest in the Pearce family.

McMurran had set out for Savannah, hoping to find among the auctioned slaves just such a family as the Pearces. He needed a family of good, capable house slaves now that his married daughter, Mary Elizabeth, had returned home from New Orleans, accompanied by her toddler son, because she suffered from a serious prolonged disease of the spine. Her mother, Mary Louise, was eager to help her daughter convalesce, but she needed help. Unfortunately for her and her daughter, McMurran had to send three of the house slaves to the Moro cotton plantation because his business partner there greatly needed them for the remainder of that year and possibly into the next. With the Pearce family having been secured for his home, however, Grace shared that McMurran must have felt a great relief that his own family's situation had been successfully put to rights.

CHAPTER SEVENTEEN

Abel listened as Grace continued her story and could see in his imagination its events and the lives of fellow human souls unfold.

After eleven days of uneventful travel from Savannah by rail and coach, Mr. McMurran arrived at Melrose, near the Mississippi River, with the Pearce family, Thaddeus, Grace, Jake, and William, in tow. For Mrs. McMurran, Grace was the most welcome of the new arrivals.

McMurran's wife, Mary Louise was a woman of average stature; her abundant auburn hair was neatly combed into a thick braid and woven from below one ear to the crown of her head to below the other ear, in soft waves that framed her pleasant features. She was of a greater kindness and fair-mindedness than most women of her station and was respected and highly regarded by the majority of her and her husband's relatives and friends, as well as by the slaves at Melrose under her husband's charge. Abel had concluded the worried mother was won over by Grace from what Grace had told him about the care she gave to Mary Elizabeth, who was very much a smaller, frail version of her mother.

Mr. McMurran's concerns, too, were probably calmed by the comfort Grace brought to his wife and daughter. As discovered by Grace, Mary Elizabeth's health had shown little improvement in the three weeks prior to his

99

return to Melrose, but her health had improved steadily under Grace's nursing care. Soon, therefore, Grace was given the responsibility for the major care of Mary Elizabeth's two-year-old son, whom all referred to as "Fazee."

Thaddeus and Jake assisted in the care of the vast gardens surrounding the manor, maintaining and repairing the house and outbuildings, and tending the livestock on the property: three goats, four pigs, three cows, four horses and a colt, and all the inhabitants of the chicken coop.

William was kept quite busy helping in the kitchen, helping his father and brother with the livestock and in the gardens, running messages from the masters to specific slaves outside and inside the manor. Frequently, the boy entertained little Fazee.

The Pearce family had been working six weeks at Melrose when, one sunny afternoon, an odd pair of visitors unexpectedly arrived. Grace had had a bit of fun describing them. The more outspoken of the pair, Mr. Q. Beauregard Humphrey, as he presented himself to Mr. and Mrs. McMurran, with Grace looking on from her nearby duties, was a middle-aged, rather short, slight man whose face was adorned by gold wire-rimmed spectacles. He wore a remarkable black, eight-inch-high top hat. Abel was amazed at Grace's extraordinary knack for detailed recall and took delight in the vivid picture she painted in his mind concerning the top hat. He envisioned the crown of the hat encircled by a three-finger wide gold ribbon enhanced by a half-centimeter of royal blue velvet just visible along the upturned edge of the brim. Unfortunately, however, Mr. Humphrey had to remove his fine hat from his balding head, thus lessening his grandeur, before entering the grand parlor, where he was escorted, along with his partner, a Mr. Frank Sims, to a large seating area.

Mr. Sims was middle-aged also but much taller and plainly clad. He slouched somewhat and wore a plain brown derby. When, in contrast to his associate, Mr. Sims removed his hat, his appearance was improved by the exposure of his well-cut, thick, graying hair.

After the two visitors had been invited to refreshments, Mr. Humphrey explained that at the same time, McMurran had become aware of the Butler slave auction to be held in Savannah, Richard Totter, a cousin of Thaddeus Pearce, also had read of the sale. Totter and his family, free blacks living in Chicago, had known that his cousin's family was among the slaves from Butler's plantation. Having heard of the famous preacher/abolitionist, Henry Ward Beecher, whose parish was in Brooklyn, New York, and who was known to have bought several slaves into freedom with funds raised from his parishioners and other abolitionists, Totter had traveled to Brooklyn to propose to Beecher that he help the Pearce family by raising funds again, this time, to buy the freedom of his cousin's family. As yet, all the slaves Beecher had been able to free were those who had been captured in the North for return to their slave-owners. Always seeking the greater profit, however, the owners often had agreed to the auctions of certain slaves at a good price in lieu of their return.

Even though Beecher had not succeeded in gaining the freedom of an entire family, Totter had begged him to try to buy the Pearce family at the Butler auction, which already had been widely publicized in advance of its set date. Totter had prevailed upon Beecher by assuring him that such an act of mercy certainly would call him to glory "when his time came," not to mention the intense interest and positive influence the publicity might have in favor of the abolitionist cause.

On that second point of drawing interest, Grace had, in her own matter-of-fact way, confirmed that Richard Totter had been correct; after four speaking engagements, Beecher had raised $5,017, well over the amount paid for most four-member slave families. Beecher then needed two capable and trustworthy representatives to go south to Savannah with the money to bid on the Pearce family and to find an attorney to draw up the emancipation papers. Humphrey and Sims had come forward with substantial credentials derived from serving Beecher successfully on several other similar, though significantly smaller, projects. The case of the Pearce family, in the ambition of its accomplishment, had been quite a new undertaking for Beecher and his attendants.

By the time Humphrey and Sims had been selected, however, the auction was to be held in six days. As their train trip was delayed by rain and mechanical problems, they did not arrive in Savannah until after 2:00 p.m. on March 3rd, the second day of the auction, according to the conversation Grace had been witness to during the visit Humphrey and Sims had paid at Melrose. Consequently, they were too late to bid for the Pearce family. Undaunted as they were, however, the two travelers determined that a man named McMurran, who owned or held interest in five cotton plantations with the combined measures of 9,600 acres of land on which about 325 slaves labored, had bought the Pearce family. Discovering through inquiry that McMurran intended to bring his newest slave family to work at Melrose, Humphrey and Sims rested only a day and a half in Savannah before heading west toward the Mississippi River at Natchez, Mississippi, by train as far as Montgomery, Alabama, then continuing on by coach to their destination.

Unfortunately, their travel was delayed once more by bad weather, flood washouts of the roads, and mechanical failures, but finally, they were brought by town coach to Melrose Manor about noon, on April 24th, precisely six weeks after the Pearce family had arrived there. The town coach entered the high, Victorian gate at the entryway of the property, followed the curving, willow-shaded roadway past the multiple acreages of lawn and well-maintained gardens, and deposited the two gentlemen at the steps of the McMurran manor.

CHAPTER EIGHTEEN

Abel tried as much as possible to adjust Grace's comfort on her bedroll so that she could rest more comfortably while speaking, which she seemed to take pleasure in doing. He playfully imagined the goings-on that hot afternoon when the two visitors arrived at Melrose Manor as detailed for him by Grace. Abel was most amused by the vision of Humphrey and Sims he was provided as the tale moved forward.

Mr. Sims took large gulps of mint juleps, first of one glass, then another, offered him by one of McMurran's house slaves in accordance with the southern plantation owner's social code. Mr. Humphrey sipped in a more proper manner from the tall glass of sweet tea with a shot of rum he had preferred as he wiped his brow with a white cotton handkerchief and continued to the matter at hand, which was, of course, the purchase of the Pearce family.

Grace shared her opinion that Humphrey's proposal had immediately angered Mr. McMurran, who, first and foremost, was a native Southerner and an owner of slaves who made his business as a plantationist possible. Moreover, he agreed with his fellow plantation owners that northern abolitionist groups were a serious threat to the South's way of life. Still, Southern custom required that McMurran treat any guest in his house with the proper Southern social grace.

Reiterating the scene in her own fashion, Grace made Abel aware of what occurred, and he felt momentarily that he had been a witness in the grand drawing-room. "Mr. and Mrs. McMurran," Humphrey stated in a loud voice after drinking the last of his sweet tea and polishing off a lemon-iced cookie. "My associate, Mr. Sims, and I do thank you for your kind hospitality." Then clearing his throat with a shallow rumble, he went on. "Ah, as mentioned, Mr. Sims and I have been charged with the godly commission of buying the freedom of all four members of the Pearce family. We were told, of course, in Savannah, about your purchase, and we are prepared to offer you the sum of $4,800 for the four. That is our proposal, Mr. and Mrs. McMurran," said Humphrey, nodding toward each of his hosts. He concluded, "Certainly it is a more than fair sum, according to our knowledge of these sorts of proceedings."

With this, Humphrey turned to Sims, who sat in a comfortable wicker chair beside the large armchair on which Humphrey had been lounging. Sims affirmed his partner's statements by lifting his glass of mint julep as if in a toast to some unseen person and, with a profound nod, unexpectedly added with a smile, "Indeed."

John McMurran and his wife looked at each other. The amused smiles held between them had faded.

After turning again toward his guests, McMurran patted his knees and rose up slow and tall. Abel pictured McMurran in his mind. His dark hair and well-groomed sideburns set off his pale, thin face and blue eyes, giving almost the impression of Southern nobility to his distinguished appearance.

As the story continued, Abel relied upon his recall of a Southern couple from Kentucky who were among the settlers he guided through the Sierra Nevada into California and with whom he frequently conversed on unimportant topics to pass the time along the journey. His keen remembrance of the way the couple spoke, although not from the Deep South, brought to life for Abel, somewhat, the reply McMurran might have given Humphrey regarding his last statement and based on what Grace had interpreted to him.

"Gentlemen," Mr. McMurran responded. "What you are enquiring about, while certainly not unheard of, has heretofore not been spoken of under this roof by either stranger or close acquaintance, so you will forgive me if I seem a trifle taken aback by your proposal. I have taken no small trouble in securing this Negro family for my home, indeed for the current special need of my wife and ill daughter, who are already benefitting from their presence since their arrival here more than a month ago. We would be most inconvenienced if they were to leave us now. Surely, in coming here, you could not have entertained great hopes that your superior's request would be honored.

Equally important, any proposed business dealings involving the sale of any of my slaves to abolitionists are anathema to me. So I must refuse your offer."

Grace brought up the fact that just after the master's eloquent response to Humphrey, a young black man, one of the house servants, approached Mrs. McMurran and whispered something to her. The mistress then excused herself and climbed the winding staircase to the second floor. "I found out a little later she'd been in with Mary Elizabeth in her room upstairs," Grace had interjected, with her listener eager to know what transpired. Abel immediately learned that several minutes after the summons from her daughter, Mrs. McMurran returned to the first floor and called to the strangers, who were being escorted through the entranceway to the front door by an elderly male house servant, to "wait a moment, please." Mr. McMurran, who was still in the parlor, had summoned a carriage and driver who waited outside to take the two men into town for the night.

Abel smiled to himself imagining Mary Louise as she hurried to her husband, gripped his sleeve, and said to him, "Perhaps, John, we are being too hasty in this decision." Then taking his arm, she gently took him aside, saying, "May I speak with you a moment, Dear?" Her husband responded by guiding her into the large study to the right of the entranceway and closing the door. At this point, Grace informed Abel, "That's when her and her husband come into the study, when I'd no sooner come in myself to dust and polish."

Mr. Humphrey and Mr. Sims, looking completely puzzled, were invited by a servant to return to their former resting places in the parlor. By this time, William had already slunk down the stairs "so's he could keep an eye on the going's on." The McMurrans did not return for almost half an hour to their waiting guests, who were apparently struck by the sudden turn of events.

Messrs. Humphrey and Sims did not know, of course, that Timothy, the young black servant, who had befriended the entire Pearce family from the day of their arrival at Melrose but who had developed an even stronger bond with William, was at his duties dusting the parlor when he overheard the visitors' request to buy the Pearce family and the reasons for that. Unnoticed by those in the parlor, he ran upstairs to the playroom where William was amusing little Fazee while Mary Elizabeth was resting in the adjoining room. Timothy quickly told William about the conversation he had heard in the parlor. Overwhelmed, William shushed his friend and led him quickly to Mary Elizabeth's room, where, taking turns, both boys relayed to her what was taking place in the parlor below.

William entreated Mary Elizabeth to pity his family, especially his mother, Grace, who had virtually "nursed you back to the land of the livin' when you was 'most gone from it." With no more prompting than this, William evidently won the clearly enthusiastic goodwill and agreement of the young mother, whose return to health and a new, decided cheerfulness was due in no small part, she obviously recognized, to Grace's assistance. Mary Elizabeth hurriedly had sent Timothy to summon her mother in order to speak to her privately on behalf of the Pearce family before the visitors had been dismissed. All of this had been communicated by William to his family later in order to satisfy their eager questions on the topic posed by his mother, "What all went on up there, son, when we was downstairs waitin' on the mistress?"

On hearing Mary Elizabeth's petition, her mother plainly felt defenseless to refuse it. She understood that pure gratitude spurred her daughter's desire for the release of the Pearce family, especially Grace, who seemingly had restored Mary Elizabeth to health when the family had held little hope for their daughter's recovery from the strange illness that had threatened her life.

While in the study, Mary Louise spoke confidentially to her husband but audibly enough so that Grace, who was within earshot, had no trouble hearing. Her presence was of no consequence to them as she went about her daily rounds. Mary Louise tried to persuade her husband that with the money offered for the purchase of the Pearce family, quite possibly as many as six good slaves could be brought to Melrose to replace them; and that, at any rate, they should not inflict such a clear disappointment on their recovering daughter, now that she had revealed her wishes in the matter.

Although his gaze softened at the mention of Mary Elizabeth, McMurran indicated that he was not convinced that even if he agreed to the sale of the Pearce family, the sum offered by Humphrey and Sims was substantial enough to cover the grievance such a transaction would effect. Mary Louise certainly knew their visitors had heated and fanned her husband's forceful pride in his Southern loyalty and, also, according to Grace, "knowing a mother's heart," obviously realized that her daughter was indeed the key to turning her husband's heart in the matter, thus, to gaining Mary Elizabeth's request. She, therefore, pursued again the reasoning of their daughter's sentiments in the matter and finally convinced him not only to agree to the sale but to take the original offer so that the sale could be concluded quickly.

Mr. McMurran conceded to emancipate the Pearce family, but with one condition: the transaction would not be completed until he had found suitable replacements.

A happy ending for the Pearces, the McMurrans, and the gentlemen from New York was achieved that evening when they learned from the elderly house servant that his own three nephews, a niece, and their mother could be bought from a neighboring Mississippi plantation owner, who, the servant had just come to know, was pressed to sell some of his better slaves to cover rising debts.

Grace punctuated the triumph in this episode of her tale. "The happy endin' was even better when we was all given our freedom papers signed by Mr. McMurran himself, him bein' a good and famous lawyer." Then Grace beckoned for a cup of water and drank down the refreshing liquid before handing the empty cup back to Abel.

CHAPTER NINETEEN

Abel marveled at the way Grace came alive while relating her history, as if she had been injected with a life-giving elixir, and he cautioned her to pause and rest at intervals. She heeded such cautions a couple of times but mostly plunged ahead with such earnest that Abel thought it a better tonic to let her continue than to suppress the soothing consolation, and even delight, it seemed to give her in relating the account of her precious family. Hence, with Abel a most willing listener, Grace proceeded with telling her story.

Again, Abel pieced together with the accuracy owing to a story well told, what Grace unfolded before him with uncanny detail. When all transactions were completed, Humphrey and Sims heartily thanked the McMurrans, then prepared themselves for the long trek back to Brooklyn. They realized before their travel plans were set, however, that the Pearces, if allowed to travel alone, would be faced not only with a difficult but a dangerous trip to Chicago, where they would join Thaddeus' cousin, Richard Totter. The greatest risk, of course, was that unscrupulous bounty hunters would waylay the Pearces soon after they left Melrose. Typically, the bounty hunters disregarded, even destroyed, the emancipation papers of a kidnapped slave and sold the slave to some equally unscrupulous plantation owner.

112

Consequently, Humphrey and Sims wisely chose to accompany and guide the Pearce family on its journey. The best route, of course, was northward via the Mississippi River on a steamboat to St. Louis, then mainly by train, on the Chicago, Alton & St. Louis Railroad, but with a few short sections of travel by coach from St. Louis to Chicago. The Pearce family had to ride in steerage on the steamboat, then in a less accommodating compartment on the train. That car was towed immediately behind the two rear cars containing, first the luggage, then the latrines; but that was better than walking or even riding horseback for 850 miles to Chicago, because they would have had to scrounge their food in a very hostile environment, and sleep out in the open, regardless of the weather.

The trip to Chicago for Humphrey, Sims and the Pearce family began on April 27th. The steamboat traveled about five miles per hour but only about fifty to seventy miles per day. By contrast, the train could cover more than 200 miles per day. Humphrey and Sims enjoyed clean air and good food served by white-coated blacks in the whites' section of the steamboat; but the Pearces, and particularly Grace, suffered greatly, packed in the lowest floor of the boat from coal smoke that leaked from the engines. Worse, their food was mainly scraps from the whites' tables, often several days old, thus neither very attractive nor palatable, but that was the fare of the black laborers on the boat as well. The travelers arrived in Chicago about two weeks after their departure from Melrose on May 10, 1859.

Once in that bustling, growing city of Chicago, on the southwestern shore of Lake Michigan, Humphrey and Sims accompanied the Pearce family to the house where Richard Totter lived with his wife, Cora, and their three daughters, aged fourteen, eleven and nine. Fortunately, Humphrey and Sims continued to accompany and lead them, because the Pearces, who had lived their entire lives on a large farm, were overwhelmed by the clamor and bustle of the city, with its streets filled with horse-drawn trucks, carts, and carriages and the buildings closely packed together—some, three and four stories high.

Before leaving them, Mr. Sims solemnly admonished the Pearce family. "Always keep your affidavits of emancipation safe and on your persons. That is of the highest importance." Then he gave them the $97 that remained after travel fares were subtracted from the $217 left over from the original $5,017 raised by Mr. Beecher. This remainder of the money was given so the family would not be destitute until Thaddeus found a job. Most of the Pearce family would remember with great fondness and honor the two men, Humphrey and Sims, as well as Henry Ward Beecher, who had been instrumental in giving them a new, free life. Jake, however, remained true to form; cynical, he openly distrusted the apparently happy circumstance gratuitously provided to him and his family by men he called "two dandy do-gooders from the North only lookin' for fame."

Thaddeus, Grace, Jake and William, exhausted by the long and arduous trip from Melrose, were relieved to have reached their destination, but even more, they were grateful to their benefactors for seeing to their safe arrival in Chicago. They were happy to be with the Totter family, who hugged the four with apparent great joy, provided them their first wholesome meal since they left Melrose, and packed them off to bed. Thaddeus and Grace occupied a very small room that Richard had added to the rear of the house, with the help of a good neighbor, in expectation of the Pearces' arrival.

Humphrey and Sims, even before they had achieved the emancipation of the Pearces but ever optimistic in their endeavors, had sent a wire to the Totters from Savannah as soon as they discovered the name and residence of the Pearces' new owner. The message sent had instructed Richard to proceed with all necessary preparations for the impending arrival of his relatives. Thus, the attached room was completed and made as homey as possible in plenty of time to receive its boarders. The boys were to bunk in the living room with blanket-beds, which they would tightly roll and lay against a wall each morning. Exhausted as they were, the Pearces slept for almost twelve hours that first night and were not disturbed.

Humphrey and Sims hurried back from Chicago by train to New York, finally completing their extraordinary trip of about 3,100 miles (almost the same distance as from New York to San Francisco) to free the Pearces. They immediately were welcomed by Mr. Beecher and the abolitionist community, and their stories fanned the flame of a growing abolitionist movement in all of New England. Indeed, their jubilation at the success of their missionary work was a true reward for their efforts.

CHAPTER TWENTY

"It's nothing short of miraculous how you and your family gained your freedom and made it all the way to Chicago, Grace." Abel lifted his hat from his head and swept a hand through his long hair to smooth it back and off the sides of his face. Knowing, however, that a painful sorrow was waiting to be released and that Grace was ready to tell it, he asked the question. "When did things go awry?"

"We made it all right." Grace pulled at her blanket to keep herself wrapped halfway as she maneuvered again into an upright position. "But a strange thing, I tell you, Abe, even as I set my first foot in that great city, I carried a heavy worry in my heart. Was the strangest thing. Didn't help none neither that Jake was always puttin' in his part: 'Things is gonna turn bad; you mark my words, Ma. Ain't nothin' good can come of the way we was freed just like that and then brought all that way up here by them two slick dandies.'"

Grace shook a pointed finger in front of Abel, mocking the dire warning of her older son. Then she brushed her hand through the air in her usual way and went on, "Ah, but that's just Jake, and it wouldn't a mattered much his goin' on 'cept for the worry that I felt myself, a worry I'd never felt 'fore that and couldn't see no reason for."

"Guess I'm fortunate," Abel said, hardly meaning to speak aloud. But then he continued. "I never experienced a foreboding, as my pa used to call them. I mean, I never felt deep inside me that something dark and dreadful was hovering near or about to happen. I can imagine that would unnerve anyone." Abel gazed compassionately at Grace. "Sounds like a heavier load than I'd have the power to carry for long."

"All alone, the power's not in us, son." Grace pointed upward with her right thumb. "We gotta give Him room, and then the power comes. Hear me on that. One way or another, He don't ever let us down when we call on Him. But we gotta move over and make room for Him."

Abel's forearms rested on his thighs with his hands clasped as he bent forward. He bowed his head, smiling. "You're extraordinary, Grace. I do believe what you say." He lifted his head to meet her candid eyes. "Still, I feel for you, under the burden of the weight you're describing. Seems the opposite's been more my experience. Life's always had an uncanny way of running into me when I'm looking the other way," he said. Then he shook his head, abandoning the unsavory topic.

Abel reached for one of the two tin cups he had set on the ground next to him before he sat down, along with his canteen and a drumstick wrapped inside a piece of brown paper. "More water, Grace?" he said, filling the cup with water from his canteen.

118

He handed her the cup, and she drank half of the water from it.

"Thank you, Abe." Grace sounded refreshed. "It wouldn't by any chance be a piece of chicken inside that brown wrapper I see there, would it now?" Grace grinned, pointing at the crumpled paper.

Abel was happy to see her appetite returning and sat with his own cup of water, enjoying that she relished her small meal, finishing off her remaining water and a full cup more. Grace wiped her mouth with a folded cloth from inside her skirt pocket and set aside her cleaned chicken bone on the paper it had been wrapped in before wiping her hands well on the small cotton towel Abel had provided. Then Abel took Grace's empty cup and set it down beside his own.

"Sorry for plunging in like that back there, Grace. I interrupted your story."

"Don't apologize. There's two of us here, ain't there? You got as much right to speak as I do. Besides, you remind me of things that need sayin' when you interrupt like that; so do it as often as you've a mind to." Grace placed her hand across Abel's forearm. "And mind you, tell that cook back at your fort, she makes chicken just the way I like it. In fact, I can't remember better." Grace winked. "Mmm, mm. All these angels flyin' 'bout." Grace smacked her lips and shook her head with grateful satisfaction.

"Now, where'd I leave off, son? Oh, yes, I was talkin' 'bout my awful dread," Grace continued.

119

"It happened 'bout nine months after we landed in Chicago; that's when my dread became real, on Wednesday, the first day of last February, to be exact. 'Course, the dock where Richard first got Thad a job like he promised, was closed for winter, with Lake Michigan part frozen; so the men were workin' at the Central Railroad freight yard loadin' and unloadin' freight at that time."

Grace lifted her gaze toward the nearby cottonwood tree, smiling. "But 'fore then, we did sure enjoy our freedom with the Totters." A captured light danced in Grace's eyes. "Last Christmas—" Grace paused and shook her head. "Never a day to match it! All of us there together, free and happy. Even my Jake come out with us that night when we all gathered 'round the Baby Jesus' manger that Thad and Richard'd built."

The remembrance brought a lovely glow to her face before shadows veiled it again. She waited a moment, clasping one of her hands softly with the other. "I studied some in the Bible 'bout St. Joseph," she went on. "He was a mighty special man; a strong protector, and his love was loyal. I speak with him often, up there in heaven, so close to the Lord's listenin' ear, and I tell him how I'm relyin' on his helpin' my Thad find his way back to us, same as he took such good care of Jesus and His mother and got 'em safe where they was s'posed to be." Abel noted the mixture of hope and anguish in her eyes and remained silent.

"Now, where was I? Oh, yes; that day— thank God, they couldn't find no place for Jake in neither of those jobs," Grace said. Abel could easily intuit the gratitude she felt at the thought that Jake, by God's mercy, was still with her. "If only things'd turned out different," she said. Pausing, she inhaled deeply and pushed out the breath as if to purge an unwelcome spirit from within. "But the Lord ain't had His full say yet, so I ain't givin' up on a good turnout." Grace stared intently at Abel. "None of us got the right to do that long as we're here. You hear me on that."

"I agree, Grace, if I take your meaning right." He was somewhat startled at her intensity.

"For good or worse, life keeps comin', Abe. And what you're made of'll make all the diff'rence," Grace concluded. She picked up the story where she left off. "That mornin' was the last I seen of my Thad. Richard was in a mighty uproar when he returned. Said Thaddeus had been taken away by slave catchers."

"But how, Grace? Richard could plainly identify Thad as a free man, and certainly many of the hands at the dock would have been his witnesses by then, as well. How could it happen?"

"You sure ain't never been very far east, have you, son?"

"No, ma'am. Between riding for the Pony and assisting settlers on the Oregon Trail, I've been as far west as Sacramento a few times, and I've been northwest to Montana, but I've not been

121

much east of right here." Abel dug the heel of his right boot lightly into the ground underneath it.

"Guess we're kinda in the same boat; I ain't never been further west than this spot right where I'm sittin'. But I sure can teach you plenty you don't know yet 'bout goin' in the other direction, and not just hearsay neither. Slave catchers are ruthless; there ain't no other word for 'em, 'less it's *mean* and *just plain Godless.*" Sparks kindled in her ebony eyes.

"And his papers, Grace?"

She nodded. "My Thad had his freedom papers on him when he left with Richard that mornin'—all three of us made sure of that, just like we did every other mornin' 'fore their pa left. Outside ourselves, them papers are the most valuable goods we possess.

"Those slave catchers don't care none 'bout legalities. If there's two or three of 'em, they can ambush a man and take his papers from him, even destroyin' the legal evidence if they've a mind to. Then they'll have him jailed until he's legally claimed by his master. Once in a while, someone'll come forward, as long as he's not a Negro, with convincin' information on the suspected runaway, and he'll be turned free. But that ain't often the case."

"Well, what good does that do the one who put the man in jail in the first place? Evil's always looking for some kind of profit as far as I've seen. I'm afraid I don't quite get it." Abel shook his head and threw up his hands in question.

"You see, when a certain amount of months go by with no one able to show no proof of freedom for the captive," Grace explained, "the slave catcher can take him, or her—they prey on the strong, fit men like my Thad; and they go after young, strong women, too, 'bout as often. The slave catcher can claim his prisoner if no one speaks up for him and sell him at auction to a plantation owner in the South. Sometimes they even capture 'em as was born free and pass 'em off as runaways to make money off of 'em. Right there's your evil man's profit, Abe."

"So you believe Thaddeus has been sold already back into slavery."

Grace nodded. "Or waitin' on it, tryin' to figure a way to escape. Can't tell where my Thad might be right now. When Richard tried to stop the two that took him, he was cut and bruised pretty bad. Cora and me took some time tendin' to him."

"Why do you suppose they didn't go for Richard, too, Grace?"

"Thad and Richard was apart from the other workers just then, as Richard told it, and I 'magine the slave catchers had their opportunity but couldn't take both of 'em at the same time. There was only two men, Richard said. And truth be told, my Thad would bring a better price than Richard at a slave auction. Richard ain't known a slave's life; 'sides, he ain't so big when you compare the two. In truth, he ain't so strong as my Thad and don't look it, plain and simple," replied Grace. "Took both them men to keep a hold of Thad, make no

123

mistake. 'Course Richard tried to help his cousin, but it weren't no use; and with no other willin' help in sight, my Thad was stolen away from me."

Abel shook his head, apprehending her logic. "Of course, they took your husband's papers, too." Disgust welled within him.

"No trace'll ever be found of 'em," Grace said, wagging an index finger.

"So there's nothing anyone can do." Frustration filled Abel.

"Tryin' to find him'd be too dangerous. We could all be caught and separated in the same manner, and likely none of us'd be seein' each other again. There's more chance of one makin' a break for freedom than four. 'Sides, there's one other thing. Richard said, 'fore them two ambushers managed to wrestle him into the back of a buckboard and ride off, Thad just kept yellin' the word, 'Sacramento.'

"Richard didn't know what he meant by callin' out like that, but I knew right away. He was signalin' me, Abe, to go ahead with our plans no matter what, and that he'd meet me if there was a way. My Thad's got a better chance at escapin' than some.

"Add to it, me and William's been keepin' him in our prayers night and day. And if it turn's out, Lord forbid, we don't see each other again in this life, leastways, we're doin' what Thad thought was best for us, and I believe he was right. We talked 'bout it, in fact, when we was together, just him and me, awake on some of those terrible, cold nights livin' there with

Richard and Cora. We couldn't be crowdin' 'em forever; 'sides we wanted to move west and make a better, safer life for ourselves, much as we could anyways. From the stories we heard, California sounded a mite more promisin' than where we was. So I knew, when Richard was so startled by the fact that all Thad kept shoutin' was the word, 'Sacramento,' that was our signal, in a word, to head there soon as possible. Only message Thad had time to get to me, the way they took him away. And there's where we'll meet, if it's to be at all."

William had mentioned his family intended to settle in Sacramento. Abel's notion to assist the Pearces on their journey there became a firm resolution in his mind, as the full plight of the Pearce family had now been revealed to him.

CHAPTER TWENTY-ONE

Grace took a moment to gather the long, loose strands of her hair in a bunch which she twisted and rolled into a bun at the back of her head, securing it with two hairpins she produced out of thin air, or so it seemed to Abel. Then she settled down and fixed her eyes on him. "And that, sir, is how we came to be in this barren strip of wilderness. We shook the dust of Chicago off our shoes 'most three months ago, and you found us here two days ago."

Abel shook his head. "You can't tell me you traveled all this way unaided by a wagon train and only two horses between the three of you."

"Seems unlikely, don't it? But that's the way it happened," returned Grace. "Mind you, Richard kept cautionin' us to wait till the end of June and better weather, but we was set on headin' out no later than mid-April, though waitin' that long was unbearable enough. Richard and Cora supplied us good 'fore we left, and we had some money saved up from Thad's work on the docks and the rail yards, plus a little saved from the money them two gentlemen from the East give us. But them two horses and a map we had was given us by Marvin Thompson, another dock worker; him and Thad became real good friends. When the nightmare occurred, and Marvin heard of my decision through Cora and his own wife, he

126

gave us the map and told us to take his only two horses, sayin' that he and his family'd make due; and not to worry none 'bout it.

"Then, while we was on our way, just this side of the Mississippi, we hit a piece of terrible weather. We found the help of a kind family by the name of Irish, livin' in a small cabin 'bout two days west of a place called Davenport, in the State of Iowa. The couple had three young ones and not much between 'em all 'cept what was necessary to survive and a heap of love; more than enough of that last one to go 'round, I'll add. They took us in and gave us what food they could and allowed us cover in their barn for more than a week till the bad weather let up. Real nice family!"

Grace showed both dimples, and her eyes squinted with her smile. "You see, Abe? God places His angels all about." She glanced around and swished a hand through the air. "And their rewards will come to 'em from His own mighty hands; you mark me on that."

"Don't you think, Grace, some people inspire angels to come out of hiding?" Abel tossed his head and winked. A random thought dismissed his smile. "It's a shame, though, 'bout your other horse being stolen."

"You're right enough; our better horse was stole by two Indians while we was sleepin', a piece back. William and Jake woke up just in time to see 'em ride off. In the rush, one of the Indians scooped up our saddle bag that had our map in it and a few food supplies, too. We still had the old mare and the rest of our supplies,

127

but it made the goin' slower, 'course. I suspect what they was specific'ly after was our good horse, and in a hurry to get it, too." Grace winced at the memory. "We did manage to get a rifle just outside Chicago. Another Negro man presented it and a box of bullets to Jake when we come outside the store with a couple supplies we still needed. He must've thought we had a little money and offered the rifle and bullets for three dollars. We give him five. Jake always slept with that rifle just under his covers. He's got it with him now, 'case he comes 'cross danger."

"Seems you would've been safer in the security of a wagon train; though I admit, things happen there, too," Abel said. "But to go it alone over open wilderness like this...."

"It was Jake, Abe. Jake's the reason we traveled on our own. First off, he said we could cut 'cross to Sacramento more direct than on the wagon train, and there was bound to be some small towns or tradin' posts 'long the way. That was cover-up; and I knew it. Main thing was, after what happened with his pa in Chicago, it was like somethin' just snapped inside him." Grace stared downward for an instant. "He swore then." Grace resumed, "he wouldn't have nothin' to do with no white man's company in gettin' us to our destination. Either we made our way west on our own with Jake, or he'd set out alone. I couldn't let my family be separated like that, not when it didn't need to happen. I seen too many families' hearts' broke into pieces from being separated by force to let mine be pulled apart willingly."

Grace shook her head. "So Jake's been leadin' us over the land, with me reading the names on the map, till our horse got stole 'long with our map." She continued, "On top of that, a couple days later, I got sick. I've always been durable for my size, but I guess it all caught up with me, and I ended up comin' down with a fever. That was more than a inconvenience, but it couldn't be helped. I couldn't go no further till I got back some strength."

Abel smiled with understanding. "Sure glad I happened on you and William when I did. When your son Jake returns, and we get back to the fort, I think I can wrangle a leave; I know at least two Pony riders who I think will cover for me. I'll see your family through to Sacramento, or at least part of the way there. I know the land fairly well and a few tricks of survival, too."

"Ain't you done enough, Abel Wheaton?" Grace objected. "Don't you have a life you ought to be tendin' to?"

"Yes, ma'am." Abel tipped his hat and grinned. "I believe that's precisely what I'm doing. And I hope you'll let me do this without taking exception. Frankly, it would be a nice break. If you allowed me to be your guide, you'd be doing me a favor, Grace—that is, if Jake can tolerate a guide who's half 'white man' and half-Indian." He smiled.

Grace lowered her head and responded, "The way things are lookin', son, you'll have to pull off some kind of miracle before either half of you can get on his good side." Grace shook her bowed head, repositioning her hands more firmly on her lap. "I'd only blame myself if somethin' happened to you. As far as I'm concerned, your skin ain't got no color, Abe; and it's your soul that shines like a rainbow, son. I know you're here to help and I ain't gonna throw that in my Maker's face like it weren't nothin'. Just be careful, promise me, Abe, if you're bound on leadin' us 'cross this terrain. I'll see what I can do 'bout my older boy."

Abel pushed his hat back and observed more plainly the disquietude in Grace's face. "Don't worry, Grace. Everything'll turn out fine," he assured her. "I've been wearing you out. You need to rest, and another treatment might be a good idea." Abel put the back of his hand against Grace's forehead. "Your fever's gone down, but you're still warmer than normal. Sorry I kept you talking so long."

"Now there's an area where I don't need no forcin'," Grace spoke up. "Me and William, both. We even get on each other's nerves at times. S'pose that happens a lot when like meets like." She paused. "But just listen to me. Here I am gettin' started again." Grace swept a hand across her forehead. "The sun's warmed up a might," she said, perusing the cloudless sky, "and seein' as I'm all talked out for now—" she winked, "—guess a little nap don't sound so bad." Grace lay back on her bedroll with her soft quilt folded down at her feet.

Abel moved to pull the quilt up. "Would you like a little covering, Grace?" No answer. Her face, heavy with fatigue, she had fallen into an unencumbered sleep. Gazing on the serene Grace, Abel felt like a gallant and grateful guardian. He drew the colorful quilt up to her shoulders. Then he rose to retrieve the canteen set apart from the other ones at the foot of Grace's bedding and emptied the remainder of the medicinal solution into the clean, black pot sitting on the cinders of the old campfire. In a couple of minutes, he had a new fire going under the pot, but he did not wait for the liquid to boil. Instead, he removed the pot from the fire as soon as it was warm enough for his purpose. Then he doused the fire with a bit of water from his other canteen. The lining strips he had used each day, together with his light green bandana, were well-rinsed early each morning at the creek by Abel before the others woke, so that now he walked over and collected the dried strips laid along one broad flat side of the rock outcrop the boys commonly leaned upon.

Abel returned to Grace, who still slept, and sat down again beside her. He placed his bandana, with the bunch of fabric strips upon it, on the ground next to him and separated one of the strips, then dipped it into the medicinal solution. Expecting that the dampened cloths would not disturb her rest but rather comfort her and aid her repose, Abel lightly wrung and placed the wide strip across her forehead.

CHAPTER TWENTY-TWO

"How's Ma?"

Abel glanced sideways. "She's doing much better, William. We were talking for a good while. She just went back to sleep a minute ago. She'll be fine, thanks to all your help. Where've you been?" Abel kept his voice low, hoping that his young friend would imitate, and William complied.

William stretched out his thin frame and pointed east and upward. "To see the view from up on top of that big rock."

"Was it worth it?"

"Never seen so much land stretched out everywhere with no one on it."

Abel nodded. "True, it can be lonely, but it's awesomely beautiful, too. Especially when you need time to yourself. You're alone but not alone, at the same time."

"Exactly! That's how I felt up there—just me and my thoughts and the Lord's wide creation!. It was sure somethin'!"

The bundle of various-sized cottonwood branches William hugged under his left arm had not escaped Abel's notice; he reached out and gave his young friend a pat on the back. "Looks like we can start those carving lessons soon. Maybe tonight after supper, I can get you started whittling by the firelight."

"All right!" William's face glowed as he set down his bundle next to the campfire pit.

"For now, do you want to do me a favor, buddy...if you're not too tuckered out from your adventure?"

"Sure, Abe. Name it."

"Would you go to the creek and fill these two canteens again, please?" Abel bent down and pulled the nearby canteens up by their straps. "We'll be needing the water soon enough for drinking and for cooking. You can take Artemis and see to her, too, if you would."

"Right," said William, reaching out to grab the canteen straps from Abel.

"Just a reminder, be careful where you walk when you dismount; some of the critters around here aren't too friendly."

"I know. One of 'em crossed by me earlier; but I been watchin' my step. Don't worry, Abe." William secured the canteen straps, one on each shoulder, and headed toward Artemis but turned again to his friend. "I'll make sure Artemis gets her oats, too." He stood, feet apart, with hands on his hips, looking equipped and prepared for a mission of the most vital importance. "Be right back."

Abel smiled. "Thanks, William. She and I'll both appreciate that."

"Right. See ya, Abe." William took off with a salute and bounded in the direction of Artemis.

Abel watched as his protégé re-saddled and set out on Artemis at a fast walk until he disappeared; he thought of the boy's youth and the wholehearted grip on life he observed in

133

him despite his scars. Twelve years old seemed to him far away, but Abel had lost much of his innocence before he was William's age, and much of the rest had disappeared by his nineteenth birthday.

Presently, his attention was drawn in another direction. Out of the corner of his eye, he saw a rabbit venture into the campsite, seemingly lost, stopping at a clump of grass here and a cluster of small rocks there, sniffing about for potential food. The thought occurred to Abel in that instant that if he could nail the creature with his knife, it would mean a nice meal for all of them on their way back to Fort Laramie. He had decided to head for the fort with Grace and William early the next morning, leaving an obviously marked trail for Jake to follow if he didn't show up before then.

Keeping the rabbit in his sights, he slowly crouched down, pulling his knife from its scabbard; then, rising, he aimed at the rabbit, which stopped momentarily, examining its would-be executioner. Caught by the creature's unexpected glance, Abel flung the knife a moment too late, missing his mark as he watched the startled rabbit scuttle away from the campground. The knife, as if defeated, had hit a stone on the ground. Abel grimaced, and, feeling disgruntled at his missed opportunity, he did not bother to retrieve the knife but turned again toward Grace to resume her treatment.

Kneeling on one knee, Abel prepared another medicinal strip and leaned over Grace as he lay the moist cloth across her neck. A chill suddenly clenched his heart as he heard a heavy clicking noise from behind, a few yards off to his left. Abel knew the sound of a rifle hammer being drawn to a full cock. With split-second precision, he dipped low and pivoted around, his pistol already gripped, but the face that flashed in front of him relieved and steadied him.

Then, lowering his eyes, he started to rise and instinctively tried to re-holster his gun; but Abel instantly was hurled backward. A chunk of fire bored into his upper chest, near his left shoulder, as his revolver dropped, a dead weight, on the ground. He was down and fighting to stay conscious. Confusion and pain clouded his mind, and his sight was darkened. Although his left arm was pinned down by the pain in his chest, Abel managed to move his right hand upward to his head. He could feel the warm wetness of blood at the back of his head where it had struck a stone lying on the ground. Forcefully blinking to restore clarity, Abel tried desperately to push himself backward away from the sound of approaching footsteps, but an ominous shadow soon loomed over him. Abel was gripped roughly by his shirt collar, and his upper body lifted from the ground. He sensed rather than saw the intense, puzzled anger of the big man who held his face close to his own.

"Why did you stop? You could've shot me and lived. Tell me why," a baritone voice demanded of his semi-conscious victim.

Abel struggled to respond but managed only one word, "Jake," before he was lowered back to the ground, complete darkness enveloping him.

CHAPTER TWENTY-THREE

When William heard the echo of a gunshot coming from the direction of the camp, he quickly slung the just-filled canteens over the saddle horn, mounted Artemis, and urged the horse to hurry the short distance back. All the fear he had managed to subdue concerning the welfare of his new friend now pumped through his racing heart. He reached the camp in time to see Abel's limp body meet the ground, still in Jake's powerful grasp.

"Abe!" William screamed as he jumped from his mount and lunged toward Jake, throwing flailing fists at him. "You killed Abe, and I'll kill you!"

Jake swung around and scooped William up by his waist, with the boy still struggling to inflict his weight's worth of mighty blows. "Hold on, Will! You know this stranger?" began Jake in a flurry of confusion. "What was he doin' with his hands on our ma? Speak up, boy! He knew my name."

William's brother was six feet four inches tall and about 240 pounds of muscular build developed over twenty-one years of mostly hard slave labor. His skin was shiny ebony, and although he shared the roundness of William's and his mother's face, no dimple danced upon either cheek when he spoke, and where William's and Grace's eyes were wide and

137

inviting, Jake peered out through narrower eyes.

"He ain't no stranger!" William shot back through sobs. "He's our friend! Abe cured Mama, and now you killed him. Let go of me!" William jerked himself free from Jake's relaxed hold and scrambled to embrace his fallen friend. With his head against Abel's chest, he continued to sob. "I told you, Abe—I told you how mean he was.—I'm so sorry!— You said you'd be watchful. You promised!" Abel stirred faintly, but the boy did not notice until he felt the light touch of a hand on his back for a moment before it slid back down to Abel's side.

"He ain't dead. Not yet," said Jake. Artemis whinnied fretfully.

"What're you carrying on for?" Jake asked him. "It's men same as him who wipe their boots on us and same as him who snatched Pa back into slavery." Artemis whinnied again when the large, strange man advanced toward her as he was speaking to William, took up the horse's loose reins, walked her to the tree at the edge of the camp, and tethered her reins on one of its branches. He removed the filled canteens from the saddle horn and held them up by the straps in a clenched fist. "He got you fetchin' the water, too, I see."

***

"You shut up now, Jake!" came Grace's hard voice. Jake turned and, lowering the canteens down beside his knee, stared at his mother's glaring eyes. Roused by the shot from her heavy slumber and dazed by the sudden, great commotion, she did not become fully aware until after William assailed his brother. She turned to gaze with pity at her younger son, who had snatched off his shirt and was huddled over Abel.

"William, come here," Grace said. When he had drawn close, she asked with urgent but tender concern, "What're you doin', son?"

"I'm gonna tear up strips the way Abe did for you, Mama. There's still some of the medicine left, but not much. I wish I knew how to make more. I should've been there when he fixed the medicine. I should've paid more attention. I should've asked questions..." His voice trailed off in sobs as his head fell gently against his mother's breast. "I thought he was dead. We can't let him die. We gotta help him, Mama," begged William.

Grace gripped William's hand. "Help me up, son." Then Grace, with William's arm supporting her, walked stiffly toward the wounded man and lowered herself to his side. As she opened his blood-soaked shirt, Abel moaned.

***

Standing just behind his mother, William cried out, "Ma, look at his chest!" William was taken aback by the hideous appearance of the wound, which was far enough from the heart not to have endangered that vital organ, but the damage was magnified by the burn scar Abel carried immediately to the right of the bullet entry. So near was the new wound to the old–now bloodied–wound that, to William, they were one. He then turned and glowered at Jake, who stood a few feet away from his fallen friend. "Look what you done to him! I hate you, Jake!" screamed William.

***

"Never mind now," Grace spoke up firmly. "We'll consider this later, but now we got to get to work treatin' Abel, so maybe he won't die. I got to do my best to get that bullet out." Grace's glance fell to Abel again, and her voice took up an immediacy as she signaled orders. "Now, William, fetch the water and put plenty in the pot there." William quickly retrieved the canteens laid at his brother's feet and began pouring the contents into the pot. "Jake'll build a fire to get it boilin'. But first, I'll need you boys to set Abe on my bedroll so's I can tend to him."

"Hold on, Ma." Jake braced his large palm before her. "I'll build your fire, but I ain't goin' no further than that. I don't want no part of that man's mendin'. He's 'most dead anyway; best if you leave him be."

Grace pierced him with a hard stare. "It was self-defense," Jake said coldly. "You need your own strength, Ma; you been weak. I rode and rode; weren't no place out there to find help or medicine. I had to get back."

"If I'm able to stand at all, Jake, it's 'cause of this young man layin' here with your bullet in him," Grace admonished him. "Now, help your brother lift him over to my mat. If we could lift him with none of your help, we'd be doin' it. Then get that fire goin' and get out of my way, if

140

that ain't too much for you. Else me and your brother'll be doin' that, too."

Grace turned toward William. He had already poured the remaining mixture Abel had fixed for Grace from the pot into Jake's empty canteen. "We'll be needin' the leftover medicine, Mama," said William, holding up his brother's canteen.

"Medicine. You keep sayin' 'medicine,'" Jake derided. "How's a man gonna make medicine out here?"

His comment was ignored, and as he made no move to help, Grace directed William and the two positioned themselves to lift Abel without Jake's help. With a defeated scowl, Jake took Grace's place by Abel and, with ease, lifted Abel's upper body while William took his legs and laid him on Grace's bedroll. Then Jake went to gather fuel for a new fire, and the pot of water was soon heating over a small but hot blaze before he distanced himself from what was taking place.

Grace searched Abel's trouser belt and the scabbard at his boot for the knife she had seen him use earlier.

Supporting himself against the nearby boulder, Jake pointed off-handedly to a shiny object lying in the dirt a few feet away. "The knife's over there," he said, not offering to retrieve it. "He tossed it there before he seen me and drew his gun on me." Jake smirked. "Had his gun in his hand plain as day, 'long with that rag he was fixin' to strangle or smother you with."

Grace did not reply but continued working.

William ran for the knife and brought it to her. "Here it is, Ma. You want me to stick it in the fire?"

"Wait, son; we need bandages." Grace pointed to the pushed-down cover at the foot of the bedroll. "We'll use the lighter cover there on my beddin'." William hurried to get it for her. "Maybe 'bout this much of the blanket'll do," Grace said, holding it at arm's length and marking off a third of it with her fingers. "Cuttin' 'bout three strips the long way; then dividin' 'em as need be," she calculated aloud.

Noticing a cool breeze settling in, Grace glanced up from her occupation. "We'll need to share a blanket tonight, William. Abe'll need to keep warm. When I'm done gettin' the bullet out, we can cover him with the rest of this blanket—should cover most of him—and I'll place my quilt on top of that." Then she indicated the covering Abel had rolled up and given her as a pillow when he had first arrived. "And I'll re-fold this other small one to make a soft place to rest his head while he mends." Almost inaudibly then, gently pushing away a swatch of Abel's hair from his face, Grace offered her prayer. "Dear Lord, spare him! Time ain't right for this one," she shook her head, "time just ain't right."

When Grace reached to take the knife from William, he drew it back. "Let me do it, Ma; I can do it. I watched Abe when he was tendin' you—when he cut the extra strips from his coat. No sense you strainin' yourself when you got me; I'll do it quick. Save your strength for the operation, Ma." Grace touched the boy's smooth cheek and smiled tenderly as she acquiesced.

As William cut up the blanket, his mother stood and approached her older son. Jake was at the same spot, leaning upright against the rock surface, with his arms folded, brooding, and watching the flames under the pot of steaming water.

Grace stepped in front of him. "Son, I'm aware Abe is a stranger to you. Don't know that I can save him, but I got to do all I can to try. But if he dies, Jake..." Grace stopped to catch his evasive eyes. "If he dies, do you realize you'll be his killer? You ain't no killer, Jake. Just full of hate and anger for how we been treated and what they done to your pa, now. This young man ain't never harmed none of us; and he was tendin' me with medicine when you got back. What scares me most, Jake, is what you might be thinkin' inside."

***

Jake narrowed his eyes, as if thoughts hidden even to him lay open before the remarkable, small woman before him. His mother continued with earnest emphasis. "What scares me most, son, is that you might be justifyin' the sufferin' of that young man with all the hurt that other white men done to us." His ma grasped his arm, but he pulled away. Grace persisted. "I hurt to see you like this, Jake; you're my son. Help me with that young man, for your own sake, if not for his."

"Leave me be, woman. Just let me alone," Jake snapped. "I can't help him!"

***

Grace dropped her arms to her sides and walked quickly and quietly away. She was met by William, who held out the bundle, with the knife palm down on top of several folded pieces of blanket. "This enough, Ma?"

"That looks fine, son," said Grace, receiving the cloths. "Now, William, take the knife over to the fire and hold it there a while to make sure it's ready."

"Yes, Ma." The boy went toward the fire. Then, crouching down, he positioned the sharp blade in the heat of the flames and reported, "The water's boilin' now, Ma."

Using part of her skirt to grip the handle of a tin cup, Grace carefully scooped some of the water from the pot into a large pan that she then set down near Abel's head, on his left side. From her pile of bandages, placed on a vacant part of the bedding, she took one of the two squares of blanket William had cut to be used as washcloths and put it into the hot water.

The knife glowed hot in the purging fire as Grace sat beside Abel and washed the wound at the back of his head with some of the cooled water; next, she pulled a long, narrow cloth from the bandage pile and drew it twice carefully around his head to cover the wound and tied the two ends of the bandage gently but securely over his forehead. Then Grace set the pan of water aside, got up, and moved back to the fire.

144

After folding up the hem of her skirt several times, Grace wrapped some of the padding around the handle of the pot, lifting it to place it near Abel's left shoulder. She took a breath and paused momentarily, examining the patient's still face. "Good. Let's get that bullet outta there, Abel." Lifting her chin, she signaled William. "Now, bring the knife, son."

Grace grasped the knife handle William held out to her. She lowered the other "washcloth" into the steaming water, then brought it out with the point of the knife, waving the cloth gently until it cooled a bit. Next, she held the knife handle in her mouth as she wrung the excess water out of the cloth onto the ground, then wiped away the blood from Abel's torn flesh as best she could in order to work more precisely on the area where the bullet had entered; but she faltered when the obvious brutality resulting in the branded "S" beside the bullet wound was clearly revealed. Grace quickly collected herself, however, and re-set her mind to her task.

Abel's breathing was slight and shallow. But the moment the point of the knife touched his wounded body, he flinched and cried out. "No! No, don't!" And he struggled as he could.

Grace held back. "William, come closer," she said with urgency, and the boy responded instantly. "Bad dreams, I reckon; we got to keep him still, son," Grace told William. "I know there ain't much weight to you, but I need you to stretch yourself 'cross Abel's middle and hold down his arms tight as you can, else I can't work at that bullet."

"He's dreamin' 'bout gettin' shot by Jake, I bet," said William, applying pressure with his two hands on Abel's right forearm while keeping the left arm pinned under his two shins, thus forming a bridge on bent knees across the patient.

"I doubt that, son. How I see it, Abe was taken by surprise when he was shot," Grace responded to William's observation. "Didn't see Jake comin'. If he'd turned 'round to face Jake, he'd of had to seen it was him. And if his gun'd been pulled like Jake tells it, I'm s'posin' Abe let his guard down and never 'spected Jake'd shoot. No, son, it came on him too fast. I believe he's in a different place altogether right now."

Grace studied William's positioning. "That looks good, son. Now pay no mind to how loud he gets; just try your best to keep him still, you hear? For his own good. I'm gonna try again. Ready?"

"Ready, Mama."

As Grace worked the knife nearer to the bullet, Abel's outcry grew fainter, and his resistance against William's hold also grew weaker.

Perspiration covered Abel's anguished face as he repeated, "Not a savage; I'm not a savage," turning his head in jerking motions from side to side. Unnerved, Grace continued with a steady hand as she sought the deeply lodged bullet.

146

William glanced from Abel's agitated face to his mother. "What do you think he means, Ma?"

"I think he means just what he's sayin', son," she replied. "He means just what he's sayin'."

Grace at last secured the bullet. By the time she had removed it, Abel had fallen back into a deep but fitful sleep. She used the rest of the medicine mixture to soak the cloth she had applied directly over the wound. This was set securely with a strip that Grace wrapped around his chest with William's help.

About an hour later, Abel seemed to be awakening, but it became apparent to his guardians almost immediately that, although his eyes were open, he was not able to distinguish reality. Most of his troubled-sounding words were meaningless to his hearers. "*Eetsa....mine hiiwes lice... Mama....Eetsa.*" This continued only a few minutes, then Abel fell silent once more.

Day slipped into evening as the deep translucent blue of the early night sky was lit by flickering stars. Abel suddenly gasped and spoke again, "Where are you? Don't leave me, Mama." Fear glazed Abel's words.

"Abe," Grace said softly, leaning close. She had remained at his side since removing the bullet.

Her gentle voice seemed momentarily to dispel his fears, but shortly he reiterated, "*Eetsa*....don't leave me."

Grace took his hand and pressed it to her cheek, then slowly laid it back at his side, and rested her own hand upon his. "I'm right here,

147

Abe. And I'm stayin' here. You just get some sleep, son. I'll take care of the rest."

***

Abel gazed into eyes he recognized as his mother's and shared words spoken to that dearest soul. "*Qe ci yew yew....thank you.... Eetsa, I love you.*" Abel's eyes wearily closed again.

CHAPTER TWENTY-FOUR

Jake stood way off by the horses during the operation, but he did not fail to hear the patient's distress, as he periodically tended the campfire, only a few feet away, while William and Grace monitored Abel's progress. Now, as evening wore on, Jake watched his brother approach the horses, both of which Jake had unsaddled, placing the gear on the ground by the tree where they were tethered. William watered them and led them out to graze beyond the campsite. When he returned with the horses, William took something from Abel's saddle pouch.

"What's that?" Jake asked. He came and stood by his brother.

"Roasted chicken. Ma needs to eat somethin'. Abe was dividin' it up amongst us earlier, but she couldn't take in but just the broth made from it, at the beginnin'. Earlier today, she ate a whole drumstick, she told me. Then after the operation and bandagin' up Abe, she only had a bite or two from our own supplies."

The boy stood quiet for a moment, staring down at the napkin covering the cooked chicken meat. "Now Abe's the one who can't eat." But William seemed to snap back with hopeful thoughts and plunked the wrapped chicken down on his opposite hand. Ma says he'll come 'round to it soon enough, now that the bullet's out." William looked up at his brother. "It'll just take time."

The bitter edge had left William's voice and was replaced by an easy, tired calmness. "Here, you want some?" He unfolded the napkin covering the chicken and offered Jake the tempting fare.

Jake tore off the chicken leg that was still intact; it looked miniature in his grasp. After two bites, he had only a chicken bone in his hand. He glanced toward the light of the campfire. "How's Ma holdin' up?" he asked, wiping a sleeve across his mouth as the two sauntered toward the campfire.

"She's all right, but it looks like her eyes are 'bout to close. I tried to tell her to go to sleep, but she won't. Just keeps her eyes on Abe. She's watchin' for a fever—says a fever's likely."

"Anythin' else you can eat in that saddlebag?"

"Yep," William replied, emphatically nodding.

"Why don't you grab yourself somethin' for now and give me what's left of the chicken; I'll go see to Ma."

"Sure. Here." William handed Jake the napkin with the chicken and headed back toward Abel's saddle pouch.

Jake stepped toward his mother and crouched down beside her as she sat tending and keeping watch on her patient. She was wrapped in the remnant of Abel's coat, which, earlier, William had brought to his mother. With much of the lining intact, it still provided substantial warmth. Jake had expected that the heat of the days would continue into warm nights as well, but the weather on the High Plains was notoriously unpredictable, and this July night clearly was cooling rapidly. He was glad William had told her to wear the coat.

Handing his mother the piece of remaining chicken, Jake placed his palm on her shoulder. "Ma, ain't you done enough? Ain't nobody gonna steal him away in the night; wouldn't be worth it."

Rising, Grace looked ready to object, but Jake motioned her to be seated again. "I just meant 'cause of his condition, is all."

Jake eyed her with a softened glance for a moment. "Anyway, Ma, I got a couple of ready-for-cookin' rabbits I hunted down this mornin', in my saddlebags. I'll go get 'em now and cook 'em over that fire there so's you can eat good and get yourself to bed for a long night's sleep. And William best do the same." As Jake started to walk toward his horse, his mother rose and followed him.

He heard the padding of her small, worn shoes on the dirt as she trailed him.

"William says you think this fella's gonna make it," Jake said when he reached his gear laying on the ground next to his horse and bent over to unstrap a bulging saddle pouch. "Guess he's luckier than most; comin' 'cross you and William out here turned out to be his savin' grace after all." Jake pulled out the rabbits from the pouch by their hind legs, stood up, and, turning, held them up before his mother

151

for a quick inspection. With the hint of a smile, he lifted a brow that begged her pride at his good catch.

Ignoring the rabbits, his mother responded, "If he hadn't' of stayed with us for three days to help me, Jake, he wouldn't be shot now; he'd likely be miles away from here and safe, with me still sick as I was or worse. That's bad luck for him, not a savin' grace."

Jake cocked his head and lowered the prize game to his side. "You're the one, Ma, always sayin' things got a way of turnin' out for the best."

"Well—" Grace paused and turned her head away. "So far, they ain't turnin' out for the best." In the next moment, however, instinct seemed to pull her back to herself as she looked up at her strong, tall son. "But he can still win the fight he's got ahead of him! Can't you see, son, he's just a young man same as you tryin' to get by in this world?"

"Not the same as me, Ma. His skin ain't black. Why are you so blind, Ma? You lived among white folks all your life, and you know what we are to 'em. They're devils, Ma; ain't got no natural souls. And the hypocrites like this one are the worst of 'em!" Jake flared up.

"You watch your words, son. Words can work more evil than any whip."

"Ma, let's not discuss this now. You need to sleep through the night like that there fella you fixed up."

"His name's Abel, Jake. And he's flesh and blood and soul, same as you and me." Grace

152

brushed her palms against her skirt. "S'pose I should understand why you can't see that," she said. She peered into Jake's face. "But a person's got to start forgivin' the past at some point, or they'll miss noticin' what's truly good and instead poison their own soul and any life left to 'em." Grace abruptly turned and headed back toward the campfire.

With two easy strides, Jake stepped out in front of her. "I see more than you think." He flashed a glaring glance at Abel, who continued in undisturbed sleep, and shot an accusing finger his way as though attempting to repuncture the wound. "That man ain't only white; he's half-savage." Jake confronted his mother, "Look at him; you think I don't know it? You and William ain't keepin' nothin' from me. I knew it soon as I looked into his face. And you believe he was waitin' on my return with good intentions?"

Jake scoffed, stepping close to the sleeping figure. "White *and* savage. If you ask me, there ain't a speck of difference between 'em; one's just as vicious as the other. If they was equal in numbers and weapons, every one of 'em down to the last child'd be slaughtered on both sides, and us, too, 'long with 'em all, 'cause we ain't nothin' but property, to be used in the white man's defense. You go 'head and save him, woman, for all the good it'll do. Five years down the road from now, maybe less, he'll be lost in the bloodshed same as us. I feel it comin', Ma. You're wearin' yourself out tryin' to change men. You'll be dead, Mama, before

153

you see fifty, and who'll care? Mr. Abel here? Or anybody like him? You ain't thinkin' clear if you think so."

"Go away from me, Jake," snapped Grace. "I'm already dead worn-out, and I mean to see this boy through the night. So let me pass, and just distance yourself from us. You know where your blanket is."

"No, Mama," Jake said. His mother's tired, questioning eyes met his. He went on. "I'm against what you're doin', and I had to speak my piece, but I'm done. I'll watch Abel there; you get some sleep. I'm the one who shot him, ain't I? Wasn't meanin' to cause you no trouble, only him."

Grace shook her head. "I'm sorry, Jake; I can't possibly trust you after all you said. I'd plain be afraid to leave him alone with you."

"Look, Ma. Listen to reason. I care 'bout you, not him. But I can't get 'round the obvious fact that you ain't gonna let yourself get better if he don't. And there's William, too. If lookin' out for this stranger's the only way of seein' the two of you don't collapse on me out of pure spite, then that's the way it's gotta be."

Jake detected hope that crept with caution into his mother's eyes. "You'll do this thing, then, Jake, for me and your brother?" she asked.

"What did I say? Now let's get over to the fire, and I'll get these rabbits cooked up. In a few minutes, you and William can eat; then I want you to get yourself a good, long sleep, Ma."

154

Jake stepped aside and, placing his free hand on his mother's back, he lightly nudged her small frame closer to the fire and the ample, old log beside it where they seated themselves as he prepared to cook. The crackling flames sent up smoldering embers that released a rich, calming, smoky wood fragrance into the still, night air. In the flickering light spread about the campsite, Jake spotted William, on the opposite side, already deeply dozing under two blankets.

CHAPTER TWENTY-FIVE

Earlier, when Jake had left William with Artemis and Abel's remaining food supply to look in on his mother, William had proceeded to fill his stomach with tempting fare from the saddle pouch: a chicken thigh, two sticks of beef jerky, a shiny, red apple, and a fourth of the remaining loaf of homemade bread that he had split apart with his fingers and thickly spread with sweet, luscious blueberry preserves, all hungrily collected from the food provisions Abel had freely shared with him the last few days. William had intended to deliver a generous share of his friend's remaining bounty to his mother and brother after he had satisfied his own appetite, but his urgent need for sleep had overtaken him before he could accomplish that good deed.

***

Jake pointed out the slumbering form. "Looks like that one, leastways, fell asleep without permission; only smart one of us. Guess we'll have to wake him when the rabbit's done." Then leaning toward his mother, he added half in fun, half-seriously, "And don't you let him steal all the covers tonight after you bed down, you hear me, Ma? You know plain well he's liable to."

She prodded Jake's sturdy side with her petite elbow and acknowledged, "I know it!" The two

156

got up and ventured nearer to the point of interest.

"Fact is, he already done it. Look!" Jake said, noticing the empty spot beside the sleeping boy was devoid of any covers. "I put my blanket on your spot, Ma, so's the two of you don't need to share. That won't never end up right anyway 'cause see, he's got both of 'em already."

"Jake, you take your blanket back; I got this here coat that's plenty warm," his mother urged.

"No, it ain't." He tugged at the two corners of his rough, cotton-cloth jacket. "I got this jacket of mine, and it's plenty." Then he cast his eyes down, muttering with muffled anger, "When I think of them Indians makin' off with our horse, our other jackets and..." He stopped himself there and looked into his mother's face again. "Anyways, you know how thick my skin is, Ma. You best take that blanket. Will and me'll be just fine."

"All right," she agreed, placing her palms against his heart. "Thank you, son."

When Jake and his mother bent down closer to the sleeping boy, William's deed of smuggling and rapturously devouring food from Abel's provisions became evident in the light of the fire playing across the upturned side of his snuggled down face.

Grace softly giggled, and turning toward her older son, she whispered, "Look, Jake, the boy's got berry jam smeared all above his lip

157

and 'cross his dimpled cheek." She giggled again, gently shaking her head.

"Sure it's jam?" Jake replied curiously, as amused as his mother at the sight of his brother's painted face.

"Just look at his smile, son. Why, no child'd be sleepin' with such a big smile of satisfaction 'less his belly was plumb full of sweet, lip-smackin' berry pie or preserves. I don't see no pie crumbs scattered 'round; must be jam." She reached down and stroked the head of her oblivious little man. "Best let him sleep, Jake; no sense in disturbin' happy, well-fed dreams. But save him some rabbit for mornin', hear?"

"Sure, Ma. There's plenty."

"Couldn't help himself." Grace smiled at the sight of William lost to all worries. Spontaneously, she turned and hugged her tall, broad son. He lifted her tear-stained face, and she spoke with new ease. "I love you somethin' powerful; you know that, don't you, Jake?"

"I know it," he replied with a slow nod. He then gently motioned for her to seat herself again over by the fire as he diligently set to work preparing a meal of one of his wild rabbits, along with warm, crumbly cornmeal biscuits with beans from their remaining provisions.

When they had eaten the satisfying supper together, Jake indicated his mother's bedding on the other side of the fire next to William. "Now go get some sleep, Mama. Ain't nothin' gonna happen to your patient."

158

"All right, Jake," she called back as she walked away from him. "But you call me if need be. Promise?"

"I promise. Now, goodnight." His mother, closely hugging herself in Abel's coat, walked over and lay down next to William. She nestled in and wrapped herself in one of the two blankets William had claimed in his sleep; then she stroked his brow and gently kissed it before placing her head back and closing her eyes. In an instant, Grace had joined William in deep slumber

Covered by the remnant blanket and Grace's quilt, the "patient" was reasonably well shielded from the cooling evening air. Jake felt his inescapable disdain for the stranger again. He rose halfway and, taking a new place on the ground, leaned against the well-worn boulder, within arm's reach of Abel, and began his watchman's role.

More than an hour passed before Jake, who was lightly dozing, heard an indistinct groan from Abel. As he raised his head to observe the injured man, he clearly could see the pain that etched Abel's face in the firelight. He put his hand to Abel's hot forehead to check for fever. This instantly summoned the remembrance in Jake's mind of the rising heat from William's body when the boy lay weak with a fever after one of his beatings at Butler's plantation. Jake swallowed and blinked back the memory as he gazed at Abel.

"Half white man or whole, it's less than what you deserve," Jake soliloquized as his insides burned. "*Much* less—for what you done to my little brother—to my pa. What *all* of you done." Jake found himself talking to the night. He pulled back from Abel and seated himself a couple of feet further away.

***

In the desert stillness, resurgence began. Out of depth and darkness rose indistinct, changing images in Abel's mind. A tender but vague woman's face, a small boy clutched in her embrace, a cabin set in the middle of a wide, green valley. These brought soothing warmth.

Without warning, a looming, shadowy figure overthrew Abel's calm and cast an icy coldness through his limbs. Abel suffocated in the helplessness that seized him. He fought to form words, or merely move a hand, anything that might put an end to the torment that gripped him; but he could not stir. He remained in this state for a time, then called out, "Pa!" and saw himself, a child, running wildly toward his father. "Pa!" he called out again, clinging to his vision as if it would empower him against destruction. But he could not reach the tall man who stood in the distance.

Sensing someone's proximity, Abel feebly extended a groping hand. "Pa, why did he shoot, Mama?—*Eetsa*, Mama. Why, Pa? Why did he shoot her?"

Anguish overwhelmed Abel's being, and his outstretched hand trembled. Now a large hand grasped Abel's. He drew strength from the firm grip, and the hand did not let go.

***

With his other hand, Jake reached for the soaked, torn cloth Grace had left in the pot of water on the ground near Abel. He squeezed the excess water from the cloth and moistened Abel's hot face and neck.

For long intervals, Jake witnessed the feverish anger and confusion brought about by Abel's delirium. Amid the stark images was a faithful father who sowed courage and love. Jake learned that he, too, was brutally taken from Abel when Abel whispered feverishly, "Pa! Shoshoni! Don't go out there...No-o-o!" His chest heaved with painful breaths. "Why! I am white, too! Kill me, too! *Baika-ne! Nawaso-hai!* Kill me now!"

Following a silent struggle, Abel's eyes opened wide, his face distraught and burning. "Impossible to live with hate...let go..." His breath was so shallow that Jake could hardly catch what was said.

He moistened Abel's face again with the cloth. "Hope your will is as strong as your pa's." Jake settled in next to Abel and closed his eyes. Greatly agitated, however, Jake did not sleep.

Moments later, Jake flinched as Abel cried out suddenly. "Pa, I'm shot! It's so dark, Pa." New fear edged his voice as he murmured weakly. Jake waited. "I can't—so tired," Abel whispered, "please—forgive me."

Dread swelled in Jake as he detected no new breath from his patient, and, without hesitation, he reached around Abel, and carefully lifting the spent young man's upper body, he drew him close. With Abel's head against him, Jake rocked the wounded man and assumed the place of his father, whose name Abel had called. "You ain't gonna die, son. There's enough fight left in you. Your ma would want you to fight. Hear me? Fight, Abe! Fight, son!"

About three a.m., Abel lapsed into a sound sleep. As he eased Abel onto his bedroll, Jake noticed that his patient's breathing was easier, but his fever had not abated.

CHAPTER TWENTY-SIX

Once Abel entered a deeper sleep, Jake, too, had drifted off gradually. Finally, just before daybreak, Jake was awakened by murmurs. He leaned his ear over Abel's lips to catch his words but none were familiar to him. *"Nunim Pist....nuna kapsisuit...."* Abel repeated long lines of another language, softly, peacefully, chant-like, until he became quiet again.

Presently, Jake, hearing movement behind him, turned around. His mother stirred, and he went to assist her. "You feelin' stronger, Ma?"

"Thank you, son; I'm fine." Standing up, she smoothed her crumpled dress. "How's our patient?" she said. Jake nodded in Abel's direction, and his mother casually turned and walked that way, but suddenly turned again. "He's not...."

"No, Mama. He'll make it." Jake walked with his mother. "He had a bad time of it for a while, though. Had me worried a minute or two." Jake stopped and rubbed his stubble-roughened cheeks, studying the ground until he felt his mother's probing gaze.

His eyebrows lifted. "I know what you think. You know, Mama, a man's prone to reveal more of his true self when he's delirious than when he's in his right mind. Can't protect his secrets."

"Looks to me like both of you done some healin'." Grace wore a relieved smile and held

163

her son in a mother's embrace. Then, bending over Abel, she placed her hand to the side of his face.

Jake saw an old glow had returned to his mother as she looked up again at him. "Appears, among other things, the two of you got a common talent for doctorin'. Fever's not gone, but it looks to be down a mite from the worst of it, I'm s'posin'."

Jake stood before his mother's loving eyes. "I'm so proud of you, son." She entwined her fingers with his and pressed them tightly before letting go.

Jake gazed out past the slumbering patient to the horizon. "I couldn't listen to you, Ma; it hurt too much to hear what you was sayin'." His voice was deep, calm, and resonant as he continued, "That fella—your Abe—he showed me a road I ain't never been down." Thoughtfully, Jake observed Abel sleeping undisturbed.

"Uh-hmm," his mother answered. "You found somethin' last night, Jacob Pearce." Her eyes were misting. "Compassion—that's the power you found, son." She fashioned a little fist and gently beat it once against his breast. "Compassion that don't discount a body's worth 'cause it can't see past the color God made 'em." Grace took a small step backward and wiped the tip of her nose with the cuff of her sleeve. Then she shook her head softly. "Ain't a soul less precious one from the other; the scoundrels, too—they can change; owin' to God, they can change."

Jake looked down into his mother's face and wiped away her tears with two wide thumb strokes. "So, Mama, what am I s'posed to do with this new power I found, huh?"

"Compassion finds its own way," she replied. "You'll find what *it* does with *you*, son, soon enough."

Jake shook his head slowly. "All I know is, I seen inside that man last night; and when I was there with him, seein' and feeling it all, it was like a deep, stuck pain of my own started lettin' go of me. Sounds strange, I know, but I don't know no other way to explain it."

"It don't sound strange at all, Jake." She bent down to lift the empty black pot on the ground beside her, then set it on the cinders of the night's fire and rose up again. "Guess we stood here long enough. We'll be needin' to scare up somethin' special for breakfast this mornin'—" His mother clasped her hands together, and went on with marked triumph in her voice, "—to celebrate God's goodness in sparin' Abel, and for your new hope, son, and His rejoinin' you safe with me and William again."

Then she took Jake's hands and looked up toward heaven with dimples deep as diamond mines. "We give You thanks, dear Lord, for all!"

Her eyes danced as they returned to earth, gleaming above the smile she exchanged with Jake. He watched his mother, delighted at her new vitality, as she caught up the loose strands of her hair and rolled and pinned them quickly back into the braided bun at the top of her head. "Plenty left of that rabbit we started in on last night, 'long with the other one we got to roast—might just be meat 'nough for the two of you boys!" She winked. "There's a start, and combinin' our leftover food supplies together with whatever William left of Abe's—should be able to ration out a breakfast from it all to fit the occasion." Grace grinned. "And 'nough for leftovers tonight and tomorrow!"

As his mother set about gathering her breakfast ingredients, Jake retrieved the second rabbit and was skewering it on the spit when she interrupted him. "You let me fix breakfast. You must be plumb exhausted, son." She shooed him away in the direction of his sleeping brother. "How 'bout scarin' William out of his sack? After we eat, it's you that best be gettin' some sleep, young man. And while you're dozin'," she went on, "William and me can go and hunt down a couple of these desert critters that's scurryin' 'bout. Make some practical use of that rifle."

"Never liked you takin' up that rifle, Ma," Jake said. "I'll be the one does the huntin'." He looked in the opposite direction and pointed off to the distance. "I seen some deers on my way back to the campsite yesterday. Wouldn't take long; I could get us one. That way we'd have meat for tonight and several days." Jake bent his head in weariness and rubbed his reddened eyes, then he covered and rubbed the nape of his neck with his other hand.

His mother threw up her hands. "I can see you're set on it. Guess the sooner, the better, so's you can get back and get the rest you're needin'. Don't worry 'bout me and William; we'll do fine. You know that well as I do."

"Yeah, guess I do. Ain't never been somethin' so small and so invincible, woman." Jake gave a tired chuckle and glanced toward William, who stirred in his sleep.

"I'll wake the boy." Jake attempted to rouse his little brother, still covered to the neck, by tapping his shoulder a couple of times.

Meanwhile, his mother reached for the pot she had set on the cinders. "I'll just take a walk to the creek to fill this pot with water for cooking. Send William after me with the canteens to fill 'em up, too," she said, starting away.

Jake reached for her arm. "Ma, you're takin' things too fast. I'll tend to the water with Will. We'll be right back."

Taking the pot from his mother, Jake bent low and roused his brother again, lightly tickling the boy's rib cage through his blanket. "C'mon, Will. We're goin' to the creek to get more water."

CHAPTER TWENTY-SEVEN

The sun brightened the horizon and stretched its dauntless rays into the high blue of the sky. William winced at the light and rubbed his eyes. He sat up, forming one word, "Abe." He swung his head in opposite directions. "How's Abe? He okay? I wanna see him. He's okay, right?" By the end of his questioning, he was standing by the blanketed form of his friend.

"He's gonna be fine, son." His mother's words calmed him. "He'll be sleepin' soundly for a time now till his fever drops a bit more."

Kneeling at Abel's side, William cast a keen gaze over his friend's mending body. "His face is so different," William observed, "like he died and went to heaven, only with life all in him still." He pointed to Abel with renewed concern. "When's he gonna wake up, Mama? Are you sure he's all right? He's so still." William pressed his ear to Abel's chest, satisfied.

"Mendin' takes time," his mother said. "Abe didn't take on just a gunshot wound, son; he survived a dangerous operation; then he was took with a bad fever most the night. Your brother seen him through the worst of it."

William peered at Jake. "You took care of Abe?"

***

"Don't stare, Will," said Jake. "Someone had to look out for him. Ma had to rest, or she'd of

168

got sick again, sure. And you, boy, what you got to say for yourself? You just filled your belly and throwed yourself there on the sack and you was out. That Abe fella, he was plumb out of his head. Who else was s'posed to look after him? That's right; I got the job. And I seen it through, too."

Jake handed William the canteens and held on to the pot. "Now, let your friend be. Didn't you hear Ma? He needs to sleep and mend. Let's go fetch the water; then you and Ma can cook breakfast while I go hunt us some *real* game."

William stood in front of his big brother with his mouth half-open.

Jake saddled his horse and secured the canteens, then helped his brother saddle up Artemis. After William had grabbed the bag of oats, both he and Jake ascended their mounts, and William guided Artemis behind the sheltering form of his big brother, who started off leading the way to the creek.

***

While the two brothers were gone, Grace had Abel try to drink water from the canteen but was unable to rouse him. "Well, Abe, water ain't the most necessary thing right now. It's healin' sleep you need; you sleep now, son," Grace mandated, even though Abel heard not a word. He remained as peaceful and deep in sleep when William and Jake returned with the water.

***

Jake gave his mother the filled canteens and cooking pot and rested a few minutes. He then shouldered his rifle and headed east toward the foothills of the mountains. True to his expectations, he was back in camp carrying a two-year-old male deer on his shoulders within an hour. In another fifteen minutes, a hind quarter was roasting over the open fire. His mother watched it and turned it from time to time so that it cooked evenly and did not burn. Jake, of course, ate the good breakfast his mother had prepared; then, half-asleep before he reached the bedding she and William had occupied the previous night, Jake was asleep almost before he was on the ground.

***

Assured that Abel would not need her, Grace and William walked back down to the creek to "set a spell and just enjoy creation and each other's company."

***

Though tired, Jake had learned to be an ever-alert sleeper, thus when Abel began murmuring again, Jake quickly awoke, and realizing that his mother and William had probably gone for a walk, he grabbed his blanket and settled himself next to the patient, who had already resumed a quiet rest. Curiosity encouraged him to remain alert that he might make some sense of Abel's intermittent murmuring, but his eyes grew heavy once more. Soon, however, Abel again took up the low, strange sounds in his sleep. Jake immediately awoke and watched his moving lips faintly pronounce the same chant-like words he had whispered earlier.

170

"Nunim Pist....nuna kapsisuit..."

Jake tried to imitate the sounds, curiously repeating them to himself. "Noonee-pisnoona-kapsi....What does it mean?" The next moment, Jake was filled with certainty that his own searching voice had entered Abel's dream, for, unexpectedly, the answer came.

"Our Father, who art in heaven, hallowed be Thy name...." Softly, methodically, Abel repeated *The Lord's Prayer* in English. Then he returned to silent rest.

Jake, eyes wide open, turned his face skyward and drank in the new light gently streaming down upon him with a tranquil warmth. Now, in this newness, he could finally sleep.

***

Abel's dreams, too, were full of light.

CHAPTER TWENTY-EIGHT

About midday, a day and a half later, Jake and his mother were sitting near the campfire pit eating their lunches of jerky, beans, and cornbread, with a fresh cup of coffee each. After rapidly devouring his meal, William had gone to the creek with the horses and the canteens, having become very responsible in the regular tending of Artemis and the Pearces' horse and the filling of the canteens.

Abel began to stir from his long, healing slumber. "Your ma's just looking out for you, William," Abel mumbled.

Both Jake and his mother laid down their spoons on the tin platters they were holding and looked over at their recuperating patient asleep on the opposite side of the campfire pit.

"S'pose he's startin' to hallucinate again?" Jake said, glancing toward his mother.

"No, son. Fever passed some time ago. No. I believe our young man's had his fill of sleepin', and he's ready to wake up and join the livin' again."

Abel continued talking in his dream. "Here, give him to me. Come with me now, and we'll set him free."

"What's he goin' on like that for then?" replied Jake.

172

"He's wakin' himself up out of his dream is all. Just wait; he'll be openin' his eyes in a second or two."

She was right.

In a few seconds, Abel slowly opened his eyes and instinctively attempted to rub them awake, but the pain in his left arm and shoulder blocked him from doing that. He moaned, and noticing two persons near him, he turned his head slowly in their direction. "What....that you, Grace?" asked Abel weakly.

"In the flesh! 'Bout time you come back to us, Abe. You sure give us some scare," she replied.

***

"Scare. Sorry, Grace." Abel lifted his head but thought better of it when a dizzying pain swarmed behind his eyes. "I don't remember what happened." Then he tried to focus on the figure sitting near Grace. "Jake?" Abel furrowed his brow, trying to force a memory, and blinked in an unsuccessful attempt to clear his blurred vision. "Too big for William," he said, trying to smile and still blinking for clarity.

"That's me." Jake's resonant voice came across deep and pleasant. Setting his platter on the ground beside him, Jake stood and stepped toward Abel, then stooped and offered him his hand.

Abel winced but tried to smile as he gripped the large palm held out to him.

"Pleased to meet you, Jake," Abel said, managing to lift himself a bit on that side. "We

173

were kind of worried you might have run into trouble out there." A wave of fatigue pushed him back down on his bedding. As Jake pulled back, Abel turned toward Grace, bewildered and confused. "I can't remember, Grace. Please tell me what happened."

"It's all right, Abe. You're gonna need a little more rest, and then we'll talk 'bout it. But you're gonna be just fine," she said.

"Man's got a right to know, Ma," Jake interrupted, and Abel lifted his weary eyes to Jake's face.

"Jake, not now," said Grace. "He's weak."

"I shot you, Abe. Thought you was a prowler. Ma mended you, and here you are. That's what happened, plain and simple," stated Jake.

Like a jolt, the scene came back to Abel. He tasted the terror again in his last fleeting thoughts after the bullet threw him to the ground and his recognition that the man with the rifle must be Jake. Strangely enough, in the next moment, Abel felt at peace. His distressing confusion had been dispersed, and he closed his eyes in sleep again.

***

"Think he heard me, Ma?"

"He heard you, son," she replied.

"Thought you said he was done with sleepin' so much."

His mother looked up at him, and the shadow of a smile came to her face. "Humph. What you said to him was a good thing. He needed to hear it. I just couldn't bring myself to tell him." She bowed her head a moment. "I 'spect he'll be wakin' up again in a little while, maybe sooner than you think."

"Hey, Ma, look what I found down at the creek!" William shouted from his mount as he rode back into camp on Artemis, leading the other horse by its reins.

She motioned him to lower his voice, but he was not paying attention. "I got me a live bullfrog!"

William whipped his left foot up over the saddle and jumped down, his shoulders hunched from holding his treasure securely with both hands under his chin as he landed on the ground. Then he held up his prize with his slender brown fingers wrapped around the smooth, white belly of the creature, its long, zig-zag legs lazily pumping, one, then the other, as Jake approached William. "See, Jake! Ain't it a beauty?"

"I see, I see. He sure 'nough is a beaut," Jake affirmed, keeping his voice low. "You got to keep it down, though, Will," he said, raising a finger to his lips. "Abe, there, just went back to sleep, and Ma don't want you wakin' him up again so soon."

"Ah!" William quietly exclaimed, lowering the frog to his abdomen. "Abe woke up when I wasn't here? And he's already sleepin' again?"

"Don't take much to wear out someone who's been hurt bad. And you know well as I do, he 'most didn't make it," Jake replied. "But Ma says she thinks he'll be comin' 'round again soon; and if you stay put for a change, you just might be here next time when he does." Jake's big hand covered the top of William's head as he laid it there and slid it down across the boy's shoulder, affectionately pulling him close. "Let's go see what Ma has to say 'bout this fella you found when she sees him up close."

William's face brightened as he looked up at Jake and lifted the bullfrog to his chin again. "Yeah!"

The brothers walked toward the campfire pit.

"Is that what you two been fussin' 'bout over there?" said Grace, in a hushed voice, sizing up the bullfrog as William held out the now limp-legged amphibian. "Umm-hmm." She appraised William's happy find. "Looks like a mighty fine specimen, but I don't want that critter 'round me or my patient, hear? If you boys wanna play with that thing, best go do it down by the creek where you found it."

Jake and William exchanged glances and, raising their eyebrows and puckering their lips simultaneously, did an about-face in the general direction of the horses again.

As the day pressed on into early evening, Jake and William returned from the creek, without the bullfrog, honoring their mother's wishes, yes, but, also, happily for William, having exhausted the many diverse pleasures intrinsic in possessing one's own bullfrog. William had deemed himself ready for a short nap but instead decided to postpone it in order to help Jake gather fuel for the fire to be used to heat the simple supper their mother was preparing for.

A fat, brown beetle crawled down from the side of the sandstone wall a few feet from the fire pit and crawled toward Abel's sleeping form. Seeing it there on the sandy ground, Grace rose from prying open a can of pork and beans and shooed the beetle into flight with her skirt and a quick stomp.

***

"That was a big one, all right," said Abel, out of the blue.

Grace looked down and saw him smiling up at her, and the little scowl of annoyance the intruding beetle had brought to her countenance was quickly replaced with a wide smile. "Bless you, you're awake, Abe! How long you aimin' to stay with us this time?"

"Hello, Grace." Abel gazed at her with eyes of gratitude. "Thank you for tending to me. You must be worn out. How long has it been?"

"Since we 'most lost you? Been three nights ago tonight." Grace sat down beside Abel and, smoothing out her dress skirt, clasped her hands in her lap.

"And it weren't just me neither, Abe; everybody helped. Jake had a big part in your recov'ry. Fact is, after the bullet was out, I couldn't do no more than pray; Jake was the one who brought you through that terrible night, settin' next to you all them hours you was so feverish and out of your head. It was him who tended you till you was quiet and able to sleep, sometime the next mornin'."

Abel absorbed her words but remained quiet.

177

"Jake said somethin' 'bout 'a man's secrets.' I don't know nothin' of what he heard you say when you was fightin' your demons, but believe me, Abe, Jake ain't the same. He couldn't do to nobody today what he done to you that night with no warrant at all. I'm sure of that." Grace spoke with a passionate intensity in her eyes. "What he done was a terrible, heartless thing, but I'm beggin' you to forgive him, Abe."

Suddenly Abel sounded the depths of her disquietude and spoke up. "Oh, Grace," he said, rolling his torso with an urgent, painful effort to prop himself and bring his left hand to rest on her woven fingers. "Grace, don't even think that. I don't hold anything against Jake. I promise you. Truthfully, though, he already got on my good side this morning." Abel grinned to lighten that worthy woman's anxiety.

Grace gripped the hand that caressed her own. "My turn again to say thank you, Abe. You're a good man," she told him, then patted the hand she held and motioned Abel to lie down again. "Best not be twistin' yourself in ev'ry direction before your body's mended proper. You lie back down there now and rest, young man; them's orders." Grace shot him a wink and a smile as she rose, brushed off her skirt, and glanced around to find her half-opened can of pork and beans. Eyeing it nearby, she resumed her earlier task as Abel closed his eyes in a peaceful rest.

Not a minute later, however, William and Jake arrived to start the fire.

178

Abel heard them as they teased each other in spite of Grace's protestations to "simmer down" and not disturb "the patient."

"They're not disturbing me, Grace. It's all right. Guess I can't sleep the rest of my life away," said Abel. "And wouldn't want to."

CHAPTER TWENTY-NINE

"Hey, Abe! You're awake! Thought I'd never get to see you with your eyes open again," William yelled.

Jake nodded a greeting and proceeded to start the fire.

William abandoned his post to sit with Abel for a while. "How you feelin', Abe?"

"It only hurts when I think about moving," answered Abel.

The boy chuckled softly. "Can I ask you a question?"

"Anything, buddy."

"Well, when me and Jake was out at the creek earlier, Jake told me you was dreamin' somethin' 'bout me 'cause he heard you say my name. Do you remember the dream, Abe?"

"Matter of fact, I do, now that you've mentioned it," said Abel. "You'd gone out again scouting for your horny toad, but this time you came back with one, only it wasn't your common, everyday horny toad. It was 'bout as big as your head, pointy spikes all over it, and it was painted just about every color of the rainbow. You just stood there holding it, looking as content as can be, but your ma, there..." Abel pointed at Grace, who was pouring two cans of beans into a pot. "She was worried that the lizard's sharp spikes were going to hurt you and told you you shouldn't keep it and that it'd be happier free anyway."

William frowned.

"Exactly your reaction in my dream, William!" Abel said. "You didn't want to release it, kept saying its spikes didn't hurt at all. The only way to convince you was to take you myself so we could set it free together. That's all I can remember of the dream. It was pretty vivid, though."

"So, we had to let it go, then. Hmm. That's funny; sounds almost like what happened this mornin' with the bullfrog, don't it, Jake?" William turned to look at his brother.

"Sure does. I was thinkin' on that myself while Abe was tellin' it. Dreams are funny things." Jake shook his head and went back to rubbing down with herbs from a small pouch the already-salted piece of meat he was preparing to cook.

William sniffed the meat and hungrily rubbed his stomach.

"Sure smells good, whatever you're putting on that meat, Jake, and it's not even on the fire yet. Deer meat?" Abel inquired.

Jake glanced up again at the mention of his name, and he nodded to Abel's question.

"Yeah, Jake come back with a deer yesterday mornin' after he went huntin'," interrupted William. "Don't know how he done it with no sleep from the night before; but now we got plenty of meat for a while. You gonna eat supper with us, Abe? You must be hungry," William said.

Abel looked at Grace and Jake. "Well, if my doctors agree to it; my stomach's a little queasy, but I don't mind trying a little beans and deer meat, rubbed down with aromatic herbs."

"And biscuits! Right, Ma?" William added.

Abel smiled.

"William, simmer down, now." Grace intervened, waving the wooden spoon in her hand. "Takes energy to eat. How's Abe gonna be able to eat if you done exhausted him with your talkin' and throwin' questions at him? 'Sides, I thought you said earlier you was fixin' to go take a nap while supper's cookin'?" Grace turned to Jake. "I'm plumb tired out myself, Jake. Think I'll go lie down a while, too, if you don't mind."

"You go 'head, Ma. I'll see to supper," Jake readily replied. Grace walked to Abel's old bedding, where she now slept, next to William. The full summer heat of the High Plains desert had returned, and the evening was warm.

***

"Come here, William, and help me drag these beddings a ways from this fire, so's we can lay down and shut our eyes for a bit," said Grace.

"Ah, Ma, but I ain't tired no more. I wanna stay and talk to Abe. He don't mind me talkin' to him."

"Abe's polite, even when he's ailin'. Somethin' you got to learn yet. If you really care 'bout your friend, you'll let him get the rest he needs," his mother said.

William's head drooped in acquiescence as he reached down and easily pulled both of the beddings several yards from the fire into the lengthening shade of another sandstone outcrop. His mother added, more softly, "'Sides, we'll be eatin' in no time. Then you can enjoy Abe's company again, and you'll both be rested." She gave her boy a hug, and the two of them settled in for a nap. William, who had professed now to be wide awake, fell asleep before his mother, who shortly joined him.

***

Abel watched as Jake placed the meat on a spit and roasted it over the flames of a well-burning fire. On the ground to his right, the other two items for the meal were prepared to heat as soon as the meat was almost ready.

Abel lay half-dozing, but perked up when he heard a sound, distant and clear. "That a bullfrog?" he said. Jake turned his head, listening.

"Yep. Sure does sound like it."

"I haven't heard one of those since I got here. You suppose it could be your brother's bullfrog?"

"Could be. We left him down by the creek where Will found him."

Abel noticed a less tense inflection in Jake's voice.

Pausing to listen again, Jake smiled. "Sure is a loud fella, ain't he? Will was mighty taken with that frog. Big guy, too! No less than a foot long with his legs stretched out." Jake measured his palms apart to illustrate for Abel the notable size of the bullfrog. Oddly, then, Jake retracted the easiness in his voice, as if all at once he

183

realized the listener. "Yeah. Well, a boy's got to have somethin' to keep his mind off the troubles 'round him."

"I don't know; if you ask me, he's got a remarkable way of not letting troubles get very far under his skin. I have to admire him for that," Abel said.

"Mm-hmm. That's Will, all right. Must admit, I admire him, too, and I'm proud he's my little brother." The big man looked at Abel. "But don't go lettin' that get out. He'll get a swelled head for sure." Jake turned the spit to brown another side of the meat. "Say…" He hesitated. "You got any brothers or sisters?"

"No, I'm alone. Guess the closest I have to a brother is William. If you don't mind sharing him," Abel said cheerily. "We hit it off from the start."

Silence ensued as Jake stirred the fire, causing red embers to float through the darkening sky.

"When Ma took the bullet out and patched you up," Jake began, "you went out of your head, Abe, sayin' things. I was right there, and I couldn't leave you, so I heard a lot." He squinted at the fire. "I know your ma's gone, and your pa, too, and I reckon it's somethin' ain't no words for, livin' with what happened to 'em. I can't say I know that feelin'. My pa was stole away from us, but we got hopes, however slim they may be, of gettin' him back. You ain't got those hopes, Abe, but I was thinkin'…I had a lot of time for thinkin' since I shot you…I been thinkin' you got other hopes, new ones. And so do I, new ones to look forward to, 'cause I ain't a slave no more, and my family is free and ain't nobody gonna take that from us."

Caught unawares and deeply struck by Jake's words, Abel quickly brushed the wetness from one side of his face. The smoky smell of the roasting meat was a calming aroma, and he managed to abate any unwitting flow of new tears. A question pressed him, though, one only Jake could answer. It should be asked now, while Grace and William still slept.

"You sleepin' again, Abe?" asked Jake as he leaned into the half-light flickering over Abel's form from the steady fire in the fire pit.

"No, Jake. I was just thinking 'bout what you said."

Jake poured four mounds of the biscuit batter into the shallow pan he held and placed the pan on the fire.

"Which part of it?" He turned the meat one more time and shaped the biscuits in the pan the best he could with the wooden spoon.

"Jake, I need you to tell me something."

Jake seemed mildly disquieted as he took the pan with the fully cooked biscuits from the fire and set it back down on the ground, then reached for the pot of beans. "Go 'head then. I'm listenin'."

"Why'd you pull the trigger?"

"You was the enemy. That's why. No other reason." Jake stopped and stared into the flames. "I'm sorry I shot you, Abe. Sorrier than you know. And I'm powerful glad Ma's prayers was answered, and you lived. What I done ain't easy to forgive...maybe impossible." Jake turned and leaned down toward Abel. "But that there's one of my new hopes, Abe—that someday I'll gain your forgiveness, and if you've a mind to accept me, right then and there, you'll gain a second brother."

Abel held Jake's gaze. "Please understand; I don't hold it against you, Jake. And there's nothing I'd like more, right here and now, than a second brother. The reason I had to ask you is that I feared the answer you gave me was the truth....that hate can rob even a good man of who he really is. I do forgive you, Jake. Please forgive yourself."

Jake set down again the pot of beans, and supporting Abel's upper body, he slightly lifted him from his bedding; then, he firmly grasped Abel's right hand with his own

"Brothers, then," said Jake. Abel gripped the good, strong hand as tightly as he could.

CHAPTER THIRTY

In the weeks that followed, Abel recuperated. For the first five days, he was well-looked-after by the Pearce family at the campsite. Later, at Fort Laramie, Grace and her boys were permitted to live there so that Grace could nurse Abel, under the army post doctor's direction, to full recovery. Abel decided to explain his injury as an accidental shooting to avoid any legal difficulties. Being seriously depleted physically as the result of his bullet wound, his second "mishap" in two months, Abel submitted to an early retirement from his duties with the Pony Express without debate. This gave him sufficient time to plan and prepare for the trip to Sacramento with Grace and her family.

Abel was ambulatory within a week after arriving at Fort Laramie; but aside from feeding and caring for Artemis, and walking her, and sometimes, later, riding the horse on short personal endurance laps around the fort, Abel had many free hours every day on his hands during his convalescence. Consequently, the post doctor loaned Abel, an avid reader as a youth, a copy of Longfellow's poems and Harriet Beecher Stowe's recent novel, *Uncle Tom's Cabin*, condemning slavery in the American South.

Another book, a historical novel set in Paris, made it to Abel's hands, to his delight. This was a copy of Charles Dickens', *A Tale of Two Cities*, hot off the press, so to speak. A rare find as yet on American soil, it was loaned to him by a young infantryman excited to share what he called, "The best story I ever read!" The soldier, having been laid up at the fort some months earlier with a disheartening injury, had greatly appreciated Abel's encouraging and sensible words to him at the time. The Dickens tale, indeed, became one of Abel's favorites, too.

During many days of idleness at the fort, however, Abel found nothing so pleasing as reading Holy Scripture, which often had been read to him by his parents as a child, and by himself as a youth. On those days, he was glad to have the Bible given to him by one of the Pony Express founders, Alexander Majors. Mr. Majors personally had given one to each of his employees with the advice that they peruse its pages often. Having lost his parents' Bible in the fire at the farm the day his father died, Abel treasured this gift from his employer; its pages re-ignited in him a fervor for God's Word. So, unlike most of the other riders he knew, he truly enjoyed rare moments when he could search its wisdom or seek its comfort. He kept the Bible inside the top drawer of the small, blue spruce nightstand, upon which he set and kept handy the other three volumes he temporarily had acquired.

Abel felt cheered and strengthened, too, by frequent visits from any or all of the Pearces, especially when they joined him just to walk and chat on his longer strolls around the several whitewashed buildings of the complex. During some of these later visits, Abel kept his promise to William of instructing him in the fine art of animal whittling, an occupation his young friend seemed to take to with unusual aptitude and remarkable precision, so that Abel knew, with pride, that the student would eventually outmatch his teacher.

Meanwhile, in the course of Abel's recuperation at the fort, Jake had been befriended by Gabe, the fort's blacksmith– beside whom even Jake looked small–and was learning the trade. Grace spent most of her time cooking and cleaning in the fort kitchen. She admired Mrs. Morris, Lieutenant Morris' wife, and the other cooks.

Her own delicious dishes brought happy reviews from the soldiers and their families, as well as from the numerous visitors to the fort.

When not practicing his whittling skills, William helped his mother with her cleaning duties, but he had not yet outgrown his proclivity for getting into trouble. These troubles, however, soon brought mostly smiles among the residents at the fort as more became acquainted with and appreciated his curiosity, charm and loving nature.

On August 15, 1860, when he felt fully strengthened and ready for the undertaking, Abel began to lead the Pearces on their long trek from southeastern Wyoming to Sacramento, California. Jake had ingeniously traded his old horse for one that more befitted his size and weight. With their supplies in tow on a mule, Grace and William rode a fresh horse given them by Lieutenant Morris; and Abel occupied a western saddle on his beloved Artemis.

***

Though tiring, their passage was largely uneventful, as though the expansive wing of a massive guardian angel hovered over the group the entire journey. Grace insisted it had been with them all along, not just on this journey. And with the surprise that met them on their second day in Sacramento, who would have been willing to deny the existence of such a guardian angel?

***

The four travelers arrived at their goal, the energetic, prospering city of Sacramento, on October 7th, and set up camp in a field near a wide stream on the eastern side of the city.

Jake sought work immediately the next day at one of the blacksmith's shops. Suffice it to say, there was no joy in Jake's history that could vaguely match the elation he felt when he recognized his father standing before him on the opposite side of the shop counter. The two powerful men sobbed in each other's embrace for a long time.

Thaddeus was, indeed, similar to Jake in outward characteristics. At six feet, three inches tall, he was about 20 lbs. lighter than

Jake and with the same dark brown skin; his dimple-less smile, however, was wide and welcoming, and he possessed much of the disarming warmth of his wife. Thaddeus quickly returned with Jake to the Pearces' camp; and, after the great joy of the reunion with Grace and William—and the introduction of Abel—had subsided a little, Thaddeus (interrupted repeatedly by Grace, Jake, and William to request clarifications and elaborations) told them the story of his capture, his escape, and his journey to Sacramento.

***

Abel listened with the rapt interest of a true family member as Thaddeus made known the intriguing details of his last several months. There was no shortage of astonishment at learning that the key player in the storyteller's escape was the Melrose plantation owner and attorney, John T. McMurran. Thaddeus, it had happened, was being held in a jail in St. Joseph, Missouri, where, coincidentally, McMurran had arrived on law business just two weeks after Thaddeus was abducted in Chicago. McMurran fortunately recognized Thaddeus, who was in a cell next to McMurran's client, as one of the four slaves he had sold and freed a few months before. He listened to Thaddeus' report of his abduction and was able to gain his release immediately by testifying in court, as an officer of the court, for him. McMurran then provided him with a replacement for the affidavit of emancipation that had been stolen from him and destroyed in Chicago.

Through astute and determined inquiry (for, as Thaddeus put it, "the man seemed overtook by pure resentment at the whole matter"), McMurran quickly discovered that Thaddeus' cousin, Richard, had planned Thaddeus' abduction and worked closely with the abducting bounty hunters well before the Pearces arrived in Chicago. Richard was in dire need of money to pay off a debt that threatened his livelihood and the safety of his family, who knew nothing of the plot then in progress. Before he returned to Melrose, McMurran forcefully admonished Thaddeus about the danger that Richard posed if he ever returned to Chicago—but Thaddeus did not intend to return there.

Thaddeus expected that his journey from St. Joseph to Sacramento would be quite difficult. Nevertheless, his hope and faith that he would ultimately find his family at the end of his journey urged him on.

Still unsatisfied, however, with the improper turnout of things, McMurran demanded that the court force the bounty hunters to provide a strong, healthy horse, a rifle and ammunition for hunting, and $100 to help assure that Thaddeus would be able to complete his journey; and, largely because of McMurran's prestige and frequent profitable dealings in the vicinity, the court agreed. McMurran, determining one further step was necessary to arrive at full self-satisfaction, then arranged for Thaddeus to join a small wagon train that was leaving in a few days. Thaddeus agreed to pay his way by serving as the hunter to supplement the group's food supplies.

His good fortune continued when he arrived on the outskirts of Sacramento at the end of August. A seventy-year-old freed black man by the name of Joseph gave him a place to live until Thaddeus could find work, then helped him to find a job as an assistant smithy at a shop not too far into town. The owner of the shop appreciated Thaddeus' quick expertise at blacksmithing, particularly as the smithy's business was thriving in the fast-expanding city.

The story culminated under one small roof, in the realization of hopes tenaciously, faithfully clung to.

Abel was sure that both he and the others experienced, that night, in the poor hovel of the shantytown, such undisturbed happiness that there did not exist in any faraway palace of the most opulent grandeur anyone who could have known the like of it. The reunited Pearce family and a new son sat together amid joyful and heartfelt exchanges with faces set aglow by the reds and yellows of firelight.

CHAPTER THIRTY-ONE

Three days after their arrival in Sacramento, Abel whisked William and Grace away on an adventure. It was morning, and the ground was still damp from the previous night's gentle rain, which pattered upon the dirt, upon the wood shanty walls and roofs, upon the canvas tents, and a rhythmic, lulling tat-tat-tattering had drummed lightly on the surface of the nearby stream. A citrus fragrance from a grove of lemon-laden trees at the water's edge a quarter-mile upstream sifted through the dust-cleansed morning air of the shantytown where Abel and the Pearces were dwelling together outside the city.

The previous day, Abel had inquired in town about the nearest Catholic church. Although at first his efforts at a boarding house, then at a mercantile store, were met with obvious disapproval, a woman who had overheard Abel's question to the clerk at the mercantile gave him the information he was seeking and directions to get to St. Rose of Lima, the only Catholic church in Sacramento at the time. It was about four miles southwest of their encampment.

Thaddeus and Jake had been at the blacksmith shop since very early but already knew of Abel's surprise plans for Grace and William that morning.

Abel had just mounted Artemis and, with William's help boosting his mother from the ground, he pulled Grace onto the saddle behind him, where she secured her arms around his waist. Everything Abel needed for his group's short journey had been packed, everything except the hat. William was about to mount the other horse.

"Got this for you, buddy." Abel reached down and placed on William's head a new tan cowboy hat with a smart black cord wrapped around the middle.

"Nah, you didn't!" William whipped off the hat to examine the beauty and newness of it, smoothing his right hand along the crease at the top and around its large, slightly upturned brim with both hands. Then he placed it back on his head and situated it one way, then another. "How do I look, Ma?" William posed before his mother.

"You look right handsome, son!" Grace replied. "Abe, you're gonna turn loose on me the most spoilt child when you leave us," she added.

"No more spoiled than I've been by your family since the accident."

"That's a kind way of puttin' it, son." Grace gripped Abel a little tighter in a brief motherly hug.

"In my book, it was an accident; you know that, Grace. We made it here together, all of us. Jake and all of you are family to me now. It's a true and good feeling I won't be giving up." Abel gently patted Grace's arms folded around him. Then, almost stealthily, he produced a folded shawl from an inside pocket of his jacket. "And this, Grace, is for you." He turned halfway around on his mount and unfolded the sky-blue, silk shawl with a patch of colorful flowers delicately embroidered in one corner and a short, yellow fringe all around that shimmered with the slightest movement.

"Ehh-h! W-what on earth, Abe?" Grace hesitantly took the gift from Abel's hands, looking at him for a moment, her black eyes twinkling with delight. "Never owned such a beautiful thing in all my life." Grace ran her hand along the soft, shiny fringe, then caressed her cheek against the blue silkiness of the shawl and gazed again at Abel, who watched with so much contentment of his own. "I ain't got no words, Abe, 'cept to say, you ain't s'posed to be spendin' what little pay you probably got left on such gifts." She slipped the lovely shawl over her shoulders, still admiring its handiwork.

"Don't you worry about my pay, Grace. Just a bit I had saved up to do with what would give me pleasure. I'm doing all right, just fine." Abel caught William's attention. "What do you think, buddy?"

"Wow! You sure do look pretty, Ma! That ain't no lie!" William studied his mother's new look with a long, low whistle. "Where'd you say we was goin', Abe?" The happy young man squinted and wrinkled his nose as he sat tall in his saddle, sporting his new hat like a peacock in full plumage.

"I didn't." There was a glint in Abel's eye as he tipped his hat back a little. "Everybody ready?"

Grace clasped her hands again around Abel's waist. "Ready," mother and son replied together.

Then Abel tugged Artemis' reins to guide the horse toward the street; he clucked and urged her eastward at a fast walk on the dirt road leading away from the shantytown.

"Is it a long ride, Mystery Man?" Grace queried.

Abel turned to answer her. "Should be there before too long at an easy pace, depending on the traffic."

"This ain't nothin' compared to Chicago," Grace said. "You been warned, 'case you ever head out that far east," and she added, "but I prefer here."

"So where're we goin', Abe?" came a voice from the rear.

"All I can tell you is that, in a way, we talked about it before, just you and I, William."

William scrunched his eyebrows together and scratched the side of his head.

"Other than that, my lips are sealed." Abel wore a wide grin as he prompted Artemis to a faster trot, the road space having opened up hosting fewer pedestrians, horseback riders, and horse-drawn carriages.

197

CHAPTER THIRTY-TWO

As they traveled, the conversation of the three riders was light and full of fun, with many guesses from William concerning their destination as he playfully announced anything that came to mind. When they had been riding about thirty-five minutes, Abel felt Grace suddenly remove her arms from around his waist. He turned his head askance, observing her quiet surprise, both her hands covering her open mouth.

"Look, Mama! He found us a church!" William pointed out the edifice as he drew his horse closer alongside Abel's. "Bet it's Cath'lic, too, huh, Abe?"

"Bet you're right," Abel acknowledged and drew in Artemis' reins, slowing her to a fast walk as they were very close to the church now. "I can't believe you had no clue where I was taking you." Abel reached toward the boy, who was riding alongside him, and playfully lifted his new hat to look under it, then plunked it back down on the boy's head.

All three dismounted from their horses and stood in front of the building whose cross-topped spire, in Abel's estimation at least, stretched upwards impressively high. From a sign that could be read from the street, they learned that being a weekday, the scheduled morning Mass had passed, and there was not another until the evening (a Mass, which sadly,

Abel realized, his friends would have been excluded from in this main church, for as yet, any black members of the congregation celebrated Masses separately, usually in a basement or annex on the church grounds, for the Church was not immune to the poison of bigotry saturating humanity at all levels).

However, one of the church's heavy, oak entrance doors had been left ajar. The trio climbed the steps leading up to the doors.

Abel stopped, removed his hat, and signaled for William to do the same. Grace pulled her new shawl over her head as Abel ushered them with a passing motion of his hat through the door he held open. No one else was inside.

Grace led, advancing up the aisle of the nave to the railing in front of the church sanctuary and its altar. A carved oak crucifix, larger than any Abel had remembered seeing, hung against the pale blue wall to which the altar was also attached. Above the crucifix, light entered from three small, elongated, stained-glass windows displaying designs of charming simplicity. From opposite sides of the nave, light streamed in through larger, plain yellow-paned, arching windows lining the soft-white walls. In either corner of the church, outside the altar rails, stood lovely, five-foot-high, hand-painted ceramic statues. On the right stood the Blessed Virgin Mary, hands pressed together in prayer; on the left was St. Joseph, carrying the Child Jesus. In front of each statue was a small, metal stand containing votive candles, each in blue or amber glass holders, creating little pools of glimmering color where many of the candles were lit. A solitary candle was lit, also, high on the right side of the sanctuary wall; its glass casing was considerably larger, shining red from the flame that flickered within.

The structure and interior of St. Rose was quite simple; even the customary transept of larger, cruciform Catholic churches was absent. Two long rows of lacquered, dark wood pews were separated by one central aisle. Though Abel had not experienced the magnificence of the Catholic churches in the east, he was, nevertheless, awash in that *presence* he had heard William speak of back at the campsite near Fort Laramie.

As Abel stood in awe, he noticed that the attention of both Grace and William, kneeling at the altar rail, was focused on the domed, ornately draped, golden box situated at the center, back of the altar.

He knelt beside Grace, as he, too, felt drawn there in an attentive, restful quiet. This peace persisted for half an hour until Grace looked toward Abel and whispered, pointing, "I think he's all prayed out." She grinned as she leaned back to reveal her lanky boy half-stretched out on the kneeling cushion asleep.

"Ready to go then, Grace?" Abel whispered, smiling back at her. She nodded. As soon as Abel and Grace had escorted William out of the church, Abel asked his drowsy companion, "Are you hungry yet?"

William perked up at once. "Sure am! Where we gonna eat?"

"Should be a park not far from here, if the woman who gave me directions was right. Got a picnic in my saddlebags; I fixed the food myself this morning," Abel said, feeling pleased with himself.

"Ah!" Grace re-situated her ample shawl about her shoulders and overlapped its ends across her heart. "I knew it weren't just the pleasant smell of lemon rinds I got a whiff of this mornin'. Abe, I had a hunch part of your secret was packed away in them saddlebags of yours." She laughed.

"To the park then!" William contributed, wasting no time hoisting himself onto his saddle.

In a matter of minutes, they were tethering their horses under the shade of a leafy willow at a nearby spacious park. There they spread out a glorious picnic and spent the rest of the afternoon in the cool shade of the willow, chattering about frivolities and discussing more serious topics, such as their visit that day to St. Rose Church, and the journeys that had brought them to the sweetness of the present, what journeys might lie ahead, and what dreams lay within. Sometime during that pleasant afternoon, Abel handed Grace a slip of paper with the rosary prayers he had written out at the fort and saved for this occasion, surprising and delighting her once more. He was certain that for himself, Grace, and William, these carefree hours together would always hold cherished memories.

201

The end of the satisfying day left Abel with rising thoughts on the Church of his baptism, the Church of his mother and his father, and of almost 2,000 years of baptized witnesses; the Church, too, that, although obviously not untouched by society's evils, up until this point in his life, was largely unexplored. He found great comfort now in its accessibility to him, like a patiently beckoning mother waiting on a beloved child's attention in order to bestow on him her centuries of measureless, ever-new treasure.

Before he closed his eyes in sleep that night, Abel breathed in deeply the mysterious, peace-filled draw of a promise he could not yet understand.

CHAPTER THIRTY-THREE

Abel rested a couple more days in Sacramento before taking his fond leave of the Pearces. He had decided to head east, past Wyoming, following Grace's suggestion. She had learned from Abel that he had indeed never traveled east beyond Wyoming. Added to this was an inexplicable ardency within that seemed to impel Abel toward the enterprise ahead.

He wondered, *Are my grandparents still living? Could I find them, and would they want me to find them? What was the East like? And what was this strange, terrifying mindset of the South that peddled flesh without a thought for the living, feeling, human souls it held captive?*

The war that he sensed would soon rage between the states was not inviting. Still, he knew too well that nothing was certain; he would head east and learn about the other half of the great land that stretched from shore to shore and meet those who peopled it, this land that, for so many reasons, was a large part of his heritage. All the while, he would search, too, the time-honored paths and spiritual wealth of his newfound Catholic faith.

The day was October 12, 1860, three months from the day he had met Grace and William in the desert; Abel's heart surged with the profound realization that his life, almost taken from him, had been greatly enriched.

Crisp, clean air mingled with that of the damp dirt where Abel and his friends had gathered in the street. He relished the feel of the good earth beneath the soles of his sturdy, worn boots and was ready to start the journey toward the pass he needed to cross in the Sierra Nevada—a route he had run more than once, with great speed, for the Pony Express.   Traveling with neither mail nor passengers, however, this run would be different.

At the hour of his impending departure, Grace, of course, wept as she hugged Abel long and tightly.

Thaddeus stepped from behind his wife and offered Abel a firm handshake. "Abe, I ain't got no words to thank you for what you done for my Grace and for bringin' my fam'ly safe, all the way to Sacramento."

"There's plenty of thanks to go 'round." Abel smiled warmly. "Don't really know whose more beholden, Thad. I only know I'm sure glad I finally got to meet you. And I'm especially glad about how things turned out." He surveyed the little group gathered there. "You all have each other again, and you're free; the way it should be."

After shaking Thaddeus' hand heartily once more, Abel turned to Jake, who stood to the left of his father, his ebony brow already glistening with tiny beads of perspiration from the hot sunlight that bathed his face. Jake reached out first and gave Abel a brotherly hug, then slapped him lightly on the back and shook his hand. "Promise me somethin', Abe."

Abel pulled back with a suspicious half-grin and squinted an eye. "Only if I can, Jake. What is it?"

"Just keep yourself out of harm's way. I ain't never met nobody runs headlong into harm the way you do, Abe. 'Fraid to say it, but William here looks tame 'longside you." They both laughed.

"I'll do my very best, 'cause that's a promise I sure would like to keep." Abel teasingly punched Jake in the arm. "Watch out for yourself, too, hear? And keep an eye on this one, will you?" he added, draping his arm about William's neck to pull him close.

"Ah, Abe, wish you could stay here forever. You'll come back this way, won't you?" William gazed fondly at his friend.

Abel's eyes misted when he noticed a tear spill, then drop from William's smooth, round cheek.

He glanced toward William's mother and searched her eyes. "What do you say, Grace? If you say it, I'll believe it; and you can bet William will, too."

She placed a gentle hand on William's shoulder and cupped his chin in her other. "He'll be back, son," she said softly. Then looking at Abel with her wide, dark eyes, she spoke with tender conviction. "You'll be back, son." She warmly embraced him once more before he mounted Artemis.

When he had hoisted himself into the saddle, Abel nodded and waved a last farewell to his new family, and tugging his horse's reins to guide her toward the trail east to Fort Laramie, he rode Artemis away.

His heart was tinged with sadness, yes, at the goodbyes, but mostly it was filled with the happiness of living in new hope. He would spend the coming winter at Fort Laramie, then continue to St. Joseph, Missouri, the eastern terminus of the Pony Express, a place he had heard much about.

Perhaps he would linger there a while before moving on if another adventure did not capture him first along the way.

In a growing inner rush of lightness, Abel spurred Artemis on to greater speed upon the well-known path. The wind whipped mane and hair as Artemis kicked up dust clouds behind them, and Abel, clutching and wildly waving his hat high in the air, sent up loud whoops that only Artemis, angels, and God could hear.

ABOUT THE AUTHOR

Alita Maria Ngo lives with her sister, two grown daughters and son-in-law in Artesia, California, a small suburb of Los Angeles County. She is a retired Catholic and public grade school teacher who also enjoyed teaching catechism to children with special needs for several years. Alita holds an M. A.in Religious Studies from Mount St. Mary's College in Los Angeles and is a member of the Secular Carmelites of the St. Joseph Province, U. S.

She was a columnist with catholicstand.com for a year, and two of her children's stories, *Harriet's Surprise* and *A Very Special May Crowning*, have been published in the Catholic children's magazine, *St. Mary's Messenger*. She loves expressing her faith through stories and is very excited about the publication of her first novel, *Good Men and Grace*, which is an historical novel set during the pre-Civil War 1800s in the United States.

One of Alita's favorite things to do is sharing early mornings over coffee and doughnuts with her sister, Annette.

Published
by Full Quiver Publishing
PO Box 244
Pakenham ON K0A2X0 Canada
www.fullquiverpublishing.com

Made in the USA
Monee, IL
29 April 2022

95103138R00125